A
Harlequin
Romance

OTHER
Harlequin Romances
by JOYCE DINGWELL

Many of these titles are available at your local bookseller,
or through the Harlequin Reader Service.

For a free catalogue listing all available Harlequin Romances,
send your name and address to:

HARLEQUIN READER SERVICE,
M.P.O. Box 707, Niagara Falls, N.Y. 14302
Canadian address: Stratford, Ontario, Canada.

or use order coupon at back of book.

A THOUSAND CANDLES

by

JOYCE DINGWELL

HARLEQUIN BOOKS
TORONTO
WINNIPEG

Original hard cover edition published in 1971
by Mills & Boon Limited, 17-19 Foley Street,
London W1A 1DR, England

© Joyce Dingwell 1971

Harlequin edition published August, 1972

SBN 373-01615-8

Printed in Canada

1615

CHAPTER ONE

DAVY's small nose pressed against the train window had changed into a squashed marshmallow. His eyes never left the passing scene, but his mouth whistled tunelessly da-da-da-da-da-da. Six da's, and Pippa knew what they meant. Almost visibly he had fondled the words when she had explained them to him, smiling back at her when she had finished: 'I like that, Pip.' Dear little boy, dear little brother, he was his father's own son when it came to expression, though ... achingly ... little use that gift would be.

She, the daughter, had taken after Mother, nothing in particular, Aunt Helen had fondly admitted to her sister, adding, 'But if you're half as sweet ...'

Pippa's own memory of her mother was vague, only to be expected when Mother had died ten years ago and she had only been ten herself. Davy had been born and Mother had died. Then, soon afterwards, Father had died, and Aunt Helen had taken the two of them, Pippa who took after her mother and was 'nothing in particular' and Davy who would have been a poet like Father if he had grown up.

Only, and Pippa looked at the small marshmallow nose, he wasn't going to have the time.

That was why she was here now. In this Australian train. Why otherwise would she have come to Australia? She had no Australian links, save Uncle Preston who was not really an uncle but her mother's and Aunt Helen's cousin, and Uncle Preston's daughter Rena.

Admittedly she knew Rena slightly. They had attended the same English school. Uncle Preston had done well in

Australia, so well that flying his daughter back and forth for her education had meant nothing at all. The identical choice of schools had been coincidence. Uncle Preston had selected it because of its prestige, but Pippa had achieved it because of an entry exam. She was not particularly smart, but she had a deep sense of responsibility, responsibility to Aunt Helen who was devoted and kind, and responsibility to Davy who was dependent and small. The selection board had said to Aunt Helen and Aunt Helen had passed it on to Pippa: 'She showed such anxiety in her papers we really felt she must have her reward.'

The reward, of course, had been only the bare subjects, no extras; they would have to be paid. There was no money to pay them, so Pippa had done without the music and dancing that most of the others ... and certainly Rena ... had enjoyed.

She remembered her first meeting with Rena.

'Has your second cousin Rena Franklin looked you up, Pippa?' Aunt Helen had asked one day.

'No, she's a boarder, and boarders and day girls don't mix much.'

'Then you must look her up. After all, you two girls are related. Then that poor child, all the way from Australia!'

Only Rena hadn't been a poor child. She had made that obvious without saying a word. When Pippa had proffered shyly: 'I'm Pippa Bromley, a kind of cousin,' proffered it humbly as well as shyly, for Rena was exceptionally pretty, exceptionally vivacious, and, even in a similar gym tunic, exceptionally exclusive, Rena had simply looked Pippa up and down and said: 'Oh.'

Looking back now Pippa smiled slightly and could not blame her. I was, she remembered, a frog of a child. Aunt Helen always had had to buy uniforms that had been

6

discarded by girls who had left and they certainly shouted it. Then those corrective glasses she had worn, so big and round! Then those rabbit's teeth behind that brace! Yes, no wonder Rena . . .

The way it is in big schools, the two had seen little of each other after that meeting. Pippa had sometimes said uncertainly, 'Hullo, Rena,' and Rena had condescended a nod in return.

Rena had been whisked away quite soon and finished in Switzerland, and that had been the end of Pippa's brief association with Mother's and Aunt Helen's cousin's child.

Yet here she was travelling to Rena's home in this Australian train!

She had been told that she and Davy would be met at the airport and driven by Rena to Tombonda, but at Mascot there had been a further message telling them to find their own way. Fortunately, Pippa learned, it was not a long distance from Sydney. Tombonda in the Southern Highlands was only a matter of some three hours, and with a fare to match. Otherwise, Pippa had thought later at Sydney's Central Railway, she might have been in a spot. It sounded ridiculous after a flight from England, but that had been Rena's gift.

Over the telephone, *London* telephone, Rena had said, 'I've seen my air agent, Pippa, and you have only to state your name.' Then she had added enthusiastically, '*And Davy's.*'

It was the undoubted keenness for Davy that had won Pippa. She might have demurred for herself, but to hear someone ask for Davy . . .

It had all started when Rena had called in at the cottage one day when Pippa was at work.

'She's in London shopping for a week or so.' – Still flitting back and forth, Pippa had envied. – 'She hap-

7

pened to be passing through our village, and decided to say hullo. I will say, Pippa,' Aunt Helen had reported, 'she was taken with Davy.'

'*Rena* was?' Pippa had been surprised.

'He's a winning little boy,' Aunt Helen had reminded her, but a little surprised herself.

Pippa had been more surprised when Rena had rung soon after and said what she had.

'Oh, Pippa,' the clear cool voice had greeted, 'would you remember me, Rena?'

'But of course, Rena. And lately, I'm told, you visited Aunt Helen.'

'Missing you, dear, but' . . . a pause . . . '*not Davy.*'

So Aunt Helen had been right. She had been interested in Davy.

'A darling little boy,' Rena had said. 'But so pale.'

'Yes.' Because she knew the end to that now, Pippa had found no words to say.

Then she had heard *Rena*'s words, Rena telling Pippa that she and Davy must come to Australia. *Soon.*

At another time she might not have listened, or at least only half listened, she might have answered politely, 'Yes, some day perhaps,' thinking 'Never at all.'

But, because of Doctor Harries, of what he had told her, had told her only this afternoon, she *had* listened. Then said: 'Yes.'

'Yes, Pippa?' Aunt Helen had looked incredulously at her niece after the phone had gone down.

'Yes, Aunt Helen. – Where is Davy?'

'Feeding the birds. He can't hear, he's at the other end of the garden.' Aunt Helen had drawn aside the curtain to show Pippa.

But Pippa had had to accept her aunt's assurance that he was out there, for she couldn't see for tears.

'What did the doctor say?' Aunt Helen had asked

quietly, but her voice had told Pippa she already knew, for they both had sensed for a long time that Davy was only on loan to them, that he was that shorter thread in the pattern of life.

'He put it gently,' Pippa had said brokenly, 'but it still meant the same. He – he said that this was the last spring.'

It was April. Pippa thought she had never known a more tender English April. Walking to the station each morning she had felt the magic ... but with it a pain beyond belief. From the leafy ledges had come the twitterings of birds, from the grass-hidden roots of bramble and hawthorn the stirrings of little creatures, dew gemmed the delicate lace the field spiders threaded on the briar. Yet Davy was not to see it again. It was the last spring.

Then Rena had rung and said what she had and standing and listening and waiting to insert a polite 'No'.... 'Thank you very much for the thought' ... Pippa had remembered that down there, down under, it was different from up here, that winter came in June, that summer came at Christmas, that autumn, never fall there for nothing fell, came when the buds were bursting here. That September, not April, was the first of spring.

September. Only five months away, and Doctor Harries had estimated around nine ... ten perhaps ...

There could be another April for Davy. April in September. September, the first of spring.

'You'll be alone when it happens,' Aunt Helen had said afterwards.

'Yes. But you do see, don't you?'

'Yes. And Rena was certainly very nice when she called, and undoubtedly she took to Davy. It should be all right. After all, she is a relation.' If there had been a note of uncertainty in Aunt Helen's voice it had only been faint. Not like the blunt warning that Janet had blurted out. Janet had been at the school, too, a kind of in-between Rena and Pippa, less extras than Rena, but certainly more than Pippa, and Janet had looked incredulously at her old friend when she had been told Pippa's plans.

'Australia! Rena Franklin! Wake up, Pip.'

'It will be all right.'

'Leopards don't change their spots.'

'I never knew Rena that much.'

'I did, and I can tell you—'

'And I can tell you,' Pippa had prevented, 'that you could be wrong. I changed. Remember the little owl I was? Or was I a rabbit? Not that I'm much different now but I don't have corrective glasses and braces any more. At least I'm different there.'

'Yes, a great deal different, and it's worrying me.' Janet had looked consideringly at the slender girl with the soft quiet face, the soft brown hair and the hillside green eyes.

'Worrying you? What on earth for?'

'Who ... or is it whom? ... not what,' had corrected Janet dourly. Then she had answered barely: 'Rena.'

'You're worrying because of Rena?'

'Yes. And I'm very sorry you're going. Why must you, Pip?'

'In Australia September is the first of spring, and Davy ... well, Davy ...'

'I see,' Janet had nodded. 'Well, good luck, Pippa.' But Janet's voice had sounded as though she strongly doubted that luck.

Pippa had gone to the air office as Rena had instructed her and the tickets had been handed over. Good-byes had been said ... if Aunt Helen had held on to Davy longer than she had to Pippa the little boy had not noticed it ...

then, with a minimum of trouble, for which Pippa mentally thanked Rena, they had set off.

Rome ... Karachi ... New Delhi ... Bangkok ... Darwin. It had gone like a dream. Only after Darwin had Pippa felt any cobweb of doubt. The brown grass far beneath them was so unending, so – so unchangeable. Did summer ever leave such terrain, she doubted, and if it didn't, and if there was no winter, how could there be spring?

Then Mascot was coming up and Pippa's cobweb was being brushed aside in the busyness of collecting bags and getting ready to be met.

Not being met had been another doubt, but at least Rena had not forgotten about them, she had left a message.

Then soon after the Southern Highlands train had left Central, had spun through suburbs whose colourlessness could have been suburban colourlessness anywhere, the cobweb had gone completely, gone in ferny hillocks, in turfed fields, in belts of green treetops, ponds of cloud-reflecting water ... most of all in the apples, pears, damsons and greengages, the medlars and walnuts that *had* to have a awakening otherwise they would not be there. That was when Pippa had happily told Davy that here 'September is the first of spring' and he had started his da-da song.

'It's like home.' Davy had unsquashed his nose for a moment to say this of the Southern Highlands and to accept a railway lunch-box sandwich. He had always been an outgoing little boy and he asked companionably of the only other traveller in their compartment: 'Is it like your home, too, sir?'

'Not on your life, cobber.' The passenger who had been reading ever since he had stepped into the compartment just as the train had moved out from Sydney folded the paper and put it down.

'Then what is your home like?' asked Davy with interest.

The man . . . large, rather too large for a narrow train compartment, Pippa thought . . . so darkly bronzed you felt yourself to be almost of a different race, began packing a pipe with such loving care that Davy forgot his sandwich to watch in fascination. The man waited until he had completed the packing to his satisfaction, then lit up and said to Davy: 'Big.'

'Big country?'

'That's it.'

'What else?' asked Davy.

'Real hills, not these pretty ups and downs they call hills down here.'

'Yes?'

'But only hills in the distance, mind you; around us is dead flat. Red, gold and purple hills. Rocks sticking out of them like bare bones.'

'Yes?'

'Flowers you've never seen before, cobber, Salvation Jane . . . though that's only a weed . . . mulga when it comes into its yellow, wild iris.'

'Yes?'

'Empty miles, burning heat, scrubbers and brumbies.'

'*Please.*' Her lips thinned, Pippa leaned across and put a slab of railway cake firmly into Davy's hand. At the same time she drew his attention to a riding school they were passing, and once more Davy's nose became a squashed marshmallow. He was thinking, she sincerely hoped, of nice dapple greys and cute chestnuts, not scrubbers and brumbies.

'Sorry if I widened the horizon,' drawled the brown man, weaving out smoke now but carefully directing it away from her.

'I'm sorry, too,' said Pippa shortly. 'When something can't be, why begin it?' She compressed her lips again.

'You have the wrong slant there,' the man answered. 'Nothing never "can't be", miss.'

'I don't wish to discuss it with you.' She took up a magazine.

'You really mean you're beaten,' he grinned. 'Oh, yes, you are. You've laid down your guns.'

'I'm reading.'

'But you've never seen a word. Look, I don't meet many people, not where I come from, so when I do meet them I like to talk. That's why I've trained it today instead of taking my car. To talk.'

'Then I'm very sorry. There are other compartments.'

'This one will do.'

She ignored him and proceeded to read, though ... maddeningly ... not seeing a word.

'Big country, you said?' The riding school was past and Davy was back again.

'That's right, little scrubber.'

'Those scrubbers, are they—?'

'They're wild cattle, wild from years in the bush. To run a steer down you have to do it in full gallop, flick it by its tail and then pin it to the ground.'

'Look, Davy,' called Pippa desperately, 'I'm sure I saw a bear in one of those trees.'

The nose became a marshmallow again and the brown man mouthed silently but unmistakably, so unmistakably Pippa could not ignore it: 'Liar.'

'I beg your pardon,' she said icily.

'So you should beg it. Liar. Rail backwards, we used to say as kids. You knew there's none down here.'

'How would I? I'm—'

'A pomegranate. Yes. But surely you'd still know koalas don't run wild any more. A few on the coast north of Sydney, some in Queensland, but not in this bit of England.'

'Bit of England?'

'It *is*, isn't it? The young scrubber just said so. Home, he said. And that's why you like it to the exclusion of any other place, isn't it? You just don't want to spread your wings. Also' ... accusingly ... 'that's why I can't widen his horizon.' A nod to Davy. 'The moment I open my mouth it's "Please.... please..."'

'Please,' said Pippa again, but frigidly, definitely, closing the subject for all time this time ... or so she thought.

For quite calmly he leaned across and took the magazine away from her, placed it face down.

'Where I come from we pass the time of day,' he told her, ignoring her indignation at his action.

'Where I come from we do, too.'

'You surprise me. I wouldn't have thought it.' He gave an impudent grin.

'What you think or don't think doesn't concern or interest me.'

'It mightn't concern you, but I bet it would interest you. Why don't you give it a go?'

'I am not interested,' she said furiously.

'The boy was.'

'*He can't be.*' The words, the aching words were out before Pippa realized it. She gave a little involuntary cry and put her hand to her mouth. Now, surely, he would leave her alone.

But not the brown man.

He said slowly, so slowly she saw at once he understood and she wondered at the intuition in such a big, tough person: 'The way I look at things you must live life as though it's lived for ever.'

'And when it isn't?' she asked in little more than a whisper.

'Then you live it all the more. – The young 'un, isn't it?'

'Yes.' She wondered why she admitted it to him, a stranger.

'Care to tell me?'

'No. I mean . . . I can't. I mean . . .'

There was a pause. 'Look.' He broke the pause. 'Look, you get back to your magazine.' He handed it to her. 'I'll give him some living for half an hour. No, don't be scared. I won't disturb him.'

'I . . .' She did not know what to say; she felt very close to tears.

'Read,' he advised, sensing the tears, and she got behind the pages, not seeing a word, only hearing his voice, then Davy's entranced little voice, then his again, Davy's, and then somewhere in the conversation, in answer to Davy who seemed since he had started that da-da song to take a lot of interest in spring: 'Sure there's spring up there, scrubber, the most spring in all the world. Well' . . . a grin . . . 'sometimes. One week the ground is stony and bare, but the next it's knee-high in grass. Then there's mulga. Wild Iris.'

'Salvation Jane,' came in Davy, knowledgeable now, 'only that's a weed. Did you know, Crag, that—'

'Crag?' Pippa put down her magazine, and the brown man explained, 'On my invitation, miss, you have to call each other something.'

'But Craig . . . he means Craig, of course.'

'Crag, not Craig. That's the name I go by.'

'Unusual.'

'Not really. It's a "met" name out west. The Crags were pioneers.'

'But Davy ... but my brother used it as a Christian name.'

The brown man smiled. 'I was baptised Clement. Me Clement! Clement Crag! Oh, no. I soon put a stop to that.'

'Did you, Mr. Crag?'

'Crag,' he invited, 'like the scrubber just said.'

'Because you *are*?' For some reason she had to bait him.

'Only in the wrong hands, in the right ones I'm pretty level going.' He looked at her and she saw that his eyes were almost the brown of his skin, more bronze than dark.

'Did you know, Crag,' Davy was trying to continue, not interested in their interchange, 'that in England, where we come from, everything is different from here? It's summer in winter and winter in summer and—'

'And it's autumn when the leaves fall,' the man said.

'Yes,' nodded Davy, 'and spring is in April.'

'And did you know,' came in the man, 'that this year you get two bites of the cherry?'

'What do you mean?'

'September is the first of spring here,' said Crag, 'so with your spring already in England you'll be having double spring.'

'At your place,' said Davy wistfully, 'it would be double double spring, because you said it's the most spring in all the world.'

'That's right, scrubber. If you and your sister feel like a bigger helping still on your plates, you come up to Falling Star.'

'Is that its name?'

'Sure is.'

'Would there be room?'

'For a scrubber your size!'

'For Pippa, too.'

'Pippa?'

'Her.' Davy indicated. 'My sister.'

'Pippa.' The man appeared to taste it. 'Our mornings at Falling Star begin at piccaninny daylight, not seven, but yes, scrubber, room for Pippa, too.'

'So you know that poem,' said Davy, pleased with his new friend. He explained of Pippa: 'She was called that because she was born at seven and had eyes like hill-sides.'

'Still has, I reckon.' The brown man was looking at Pippa, and, embarrassed, she looked away.

'Also,' continued Davy importantly, 'our father was a poet.'

'Then that settles it. A poet's son would have to come to Yantumara.'

'Is that Falling Star?'

'Sure is.'

'We're going to Tombonda,' grieved Davy.

'That means a hill. I'm going, too.'

Pippa's mouth, open to say as quietly but as finally as she could, not to put such wild ideas as going up north to a cattle station ... it sounded like cattle ... into the boy, closed again. Going to Tombonda, too!

'But that's not your country,' Davy was protesting jealously, jealous for the country he had just heard about, 'you're scrubbers and brumbies and—'

'So was my father's country until he got too old to run a steer down at full gallop, and then—'

'Flick it by its tail and pin it to the ground.'

'Yes,' nodded the brown man. 'So he came here for a rest.'

'And you've come down to see him, Crag?'

'Not any more, scrubber. He sees it all at the one time now from a good viewing cloud up there. No, I've come to

17

check the place, and to' ... He stopped. Presently he said, 'Look, Davy, there's a wombat for you.' As the nose became a marshmallow again, the man turned to Pippa and finished: 'And I've come to ask that girl next door what gives. Because' ... paying no attention to Pippa's implied uninterest ... 'when I come to Tombonda when I'm old I want someone carrying on, like I did for my father, up at Falling Star.' He stopped. 'Do you follow?'

'It doesn't concern me,' Pippa said coldly.

'But do you see?'

'It doesn't concern me,' she said again.

Another pause ... then again he broke it.

'Then would it concern you if I asked *you* to come instead?' He was attending his pipe again, not looking at her.

'What?' Pippa sat straight up.

'Because,' he went on, '*she* isn't coming or she would have been there by this time, and time runs out.' He said it quite unabashed.

'Are you the same person who just quoted that we live for ever?' Pippa demanded, still taken aback by his impudent proposal. 'Are you saying instead now that time runs out?'

'No,' he answered, 'but I am saying that the time for living life as it should be lived runs out, Pippa.' – Pippa, indeed! – 'That that right design, God's design, of man and woman, then later' ... a significant nod in Davy's direction ... 'has to have its start.'

He was unbelievable. The subject was unbelievable.

'With Davy,' she inserted incredulously at last, 'assuming that children are your theme—'

'They are.'

'You'd overcome time.' Really, she froze, this person ...

'That was what I was thinking,' he nodded frankly, '. family readymade.'

'But not for long.' She bit on her lip as the words escaped her.

He held up a big hand cancelling what she had said, cancelling it so definitely she almost could have believed him. Only, of course, she mustn't . . .

'Besides,' he resumed, 'I've quite taken to the little scrubber. So after I see Rena—'

'Rena?' she gasped.

'That's where you're going, isn't it? Franklins. Has to be, it's the only other property at Tombonda. The rest of the district consists of railway cottages and a few shops.' He looked musingly at her for a few moments. 'You know, Pippa,' he shrugged, 'you being here makes sense, or at least the young scrubber does.' He gave a short laugh.

'I don't understand,' Pippa said.

'Well, I hope you keep that up. It's not a good understanding, I reckon. – Tombonda's the next stop. Only short intervals down here. Not like our part of the world.'

'The big country?' Davy was back with them again.

'That's right, scrubber. There we don't deal in miles but thousands of square ones. Gear ready? We get off now.' The brown man was swinging the bags down, swinging Davy down, swinging . . . and Pippa rankled but had to comply . . . Davy's sister.

There were two cars waiting beyond the small neat station, one empty, the other attended and ready to go. The first was a distinctly muddy landrover that looked as though it had seen a lot of action. The other was a well-polished sedan that looked like Rena. Pippa was not surprised when a driver came forward from the sedan and claimed them.

Crag ... a ridiculous name ... went to the jeep and stepped into it without opening a door. He did not move off until after they had moved. In the rear vision mirror Pippa watched him behind them. He followed until their car swept at length into Uncle Preston's park-like property on the station side of a wooded hill.

The driver, seeing the direction of Pippa's gaze, said: 'Crag's is on the other side, and that's Crag now, he comes down now and then.'

'From the big country,' said Davy.

'That's right. Miss Rena meant to meet you today, miss, but at the last minute her father wasn't the best.'

'It didn't matter, we enjoyed the train.'

'Yes, and we met Crag,' Davy put in.

The driver looked as though he was going to say something, but evidently he changed his mind. He was emerging from an avenue of camphor laurels now and coming to a halt. The halt was by a large, dark-red brick, two-storeyed house named Uplands. It was the sort of house that Pippa rather had imagined as Rena's background – rich-looking, prosperous. The perfect scene for the girl now coming out of the front door and down the steps to meet them. Second cousin Rena. Very little different really from the attractive, somehow exclusive even in gym tunic Rena who had condescended now and then at school to smile and nod.

But she was smiling winningly now, running to welcome them ... except that the smile stiffened when she turned at last from Davy to Pippa, and slowly, estimatingly, consideringly looked Pippa up and down.

'You've changed,' Rena said.

Helping the driver with the bags, Pippa heard herself babbling about the corrective glasses having corrected, the brace having braced, and she wondered why she was being apologetic. Anyone would think I'd become a swan from a duckling, she thought wryly, whereas I'm simply a little less the owl and the rabbit than I used to be. It occurred to her ludicrously that she was using up a lot of creatures, and she gave a little laugh, but Rena did not laugh back. She was still looking her over, but when Pippa turned directly on her, feeling rather embarrassed by the close regard, to make some diverting . . . she hoped . . . remark, her second cousin went up the stairs and stood for a few moments talking to an elderly gentleman who had come out on the patio to watch them.

That they were speaking of her was obvious by the quick flick of Rena's eyes in her direction again, then a shrug and a nod from the man.

He was thick-set and stolid, but something about the features acclaimed Rena to be his daughter.

'Uncle Preston.' Pippa prompted herself to go up the steps to the man and hold out her hand.

'None of that, m'dear.' He smiled expansively at her. 'We're kin, remember.' His eyes roved over her.

'Far off,' she said faintly, not liking his rather un-uncle look.

'Not too far for this.' He kissed her appreciatively, his daughter looking on with cool amusement.

'When you're ready, Pippa,' she said, 'Daddy will show you where you're to sleep.' Her glance went briefly to him.

Pippa turned back for Davy, but Uncle Preston had his hand under her elbow and was guiding her forward, squeezing her arm jocularly every now and then. Something seemed to be amusing him and he chuckled to himself.

'That took some of the wind out of her sails,' he ho-ho'd. 'But' . . . proudly . . . 'being my Rena she soon showed who's Miss Fixit.'

For some distasteful reason she could not have put a finger on, Pippa did not ask the obvious questions. She permitted herself to be propelled up a wide staircase, then along a passage to a back room, for most obviously and most indisputably it *was* a back room.

She did not mind that. After all, she had had back rooms all her life. Indeed, all Aunt Helen's rooms could have been classed as back rooms, their old cottage being small and cheap as it was.

But this room fairly cried out back room. It was as bare as a ward and held only a bed, a chest of drawers and a chair. The window was narrow and it missed the rural loveliness of the Southern Highlands, that treesy, hillocky charm that could have been home. Instead it looked down on an incinerator, several waste-bins, a mulch heap and a woodpile. Also quite unmistakably the room ... now Pippa had turned back from the window ... had not been prepared.

Uncle Preston was chuckling again; again he was looking Pippa up and down.

'What's she like? That's what I asked her.' He ho-ho'd once more. He came nearer to Pippa. 'Do you know what she said?'

'What, Uncle Preston?'

'Do you know what that know-all girl of mine said? She said "Oh, just a little brown thing." '

'Well, I have brown hair,' Pippa said sensitively, not liking being the pivot of his attention.

'Yes, and you're small. But good things come in little packets, m'dear, and those eyes! And that sweet little face! Did I say welcome?' He leaned over, but Pippa prevented quickly, 'Yes, Uncle, you did.'

He was easy to divert, thank goodness. He started chuckling over Rena again, whom obviously he both doted on and quarrelled with. 'Didn't expect a winner like you. That'll upset her applecart.'

'I'm not.' In an inspiration Pippa added, 'I mean not like your daughter.'

They were the right words. Uncle Preston expanded visibly and agreed, 'No. My Rena's got it, hasn't she? So she should, she's had a fortune spent on her.'

He was extremely proud of Rena, Pippa decided, but he would often disagree with her for the simple reason that they would be one of a sort, the sort, Pippa thought a little sinkingly, that years ago, and she recalled it now, Aunt Helen, usually the most discreet of people, had said: 'Not the side of the family you want for yourself.'

The arguments the pair must frequently have staged were proved in Uncle's next words.

'A fortune,' he growled resentfully, 'but fortunes run out, and if she keeps on with this silly whim she's got now. . . . That's why you're put here, girl. Tucked safely away where you can't be seen.' He waved his arm round the room. 'She didn't expect you to be like you are. Oh, yes, I know my daughter.'

'It's quite sufficient,' said Pippa of the room, 'but where is Davy's? I always sleep near Davy.'

'Not necessary any more, Pippa.' Rena had joined them and at once her glorious golden colouring lit up the drab interior. Pippa saw Uncle Preston looking adoringly at his only child.

'I am taking over from you, pet,' Rena said smilingly but definitely. 'Poor little Pippa, tied down all these years.'

'It hasn't been a tie, Rena, and I would prefer—'

'But she's not going to, is she, Daddy?' A quick sharp look at her father. 'She's going to relax. I am having darling Davy near me. No, no more words. Our little Martha has done her share of work. Unpack your things, pet, and then come down to tea.'

23

Pippa stood for quite a while after Rena and her father had left. Her impulse was to go after them and have an understanding at once, tell them that Davy was *her* responsibility, that—

But it seemed rude. They had paid the fares out, expensive fares, they had taken them under their roof. Not that Pippa's corner was an attractive one, indeed it was quite unattractive, but it was still not costing a penny, and Rena was certainly taken up with Davy.

She was glad after she had placed her things and gone down that she had not insisted on that understanding. Rena stood at the bottom of the stairs and she took Pippa's arm and led her to a suite.

Davy was sitting on a padded window bench playing with an expensive mechanical toy, and while he was so absorbed, Pippa let her glance rove round. She would have been unfair had she not allowed a cry of pleasure. The room was perfect for a boy. The furnishings were many-coloured, but brightly and youthfully so. The pictures were pictures boys liked. Not only these, but Rena had shown nursing sense in including a divan as well as a bed, almost as if she had known that a delicate child must rest other hours than the expected night hours.

There were plenty of cupboards for books and toys and the wide-flung windows were cheerfully curtained.

'Rena, it's perfect! Quite perfect.'

'It should be,' grumbled Uncle Preston, who had come behind them, 'not only cost me a packet to renovate but I had to pay a nurse as well for advice.'

'Daddy, be quiet!' Rena sounded annoyed; she probably wanted the praise for the arrangement for herself, but Pippa felt a warmth for her second cousin for going to the trouble of seeking skilled advice.

'This was where you were to be,' Uncle Preston was saying, nodding to an adjoining room, which, though no larger, was much more attractive than the room upstairs. 'That's what you get for not being that little brown thing, m'dear.'

'We'll have tea,' Rena said abruptly. She gave her father a hard stare and he said no more.

A maid brought tea and cakes to the patio. Uncle Preston criticized the cakes as he munched them, saying they must have cost a few pennies to make 'with that butter and all'.

'My father is mean,' said Rena quite coolly. 'He counts the cents.'

'If I hadn't, young woman, you wouldn't be where you are. Then where's that, anyway? Hanging up your hat to a—'

'*Daddy!*'

Uncle Preston was silenced. But not for long. He explained to Pippa how thrift had got him on in the world.

'I started in business as a boy, and then—'

'Then you're not a farmer, Uncle Preston?' Pippa looked beyond the patio to the rural setting.

'Lord, no, I only bought Uplands because her ladyship—'

'That's enough, Daddy!' Rena gave another of her hard stares.

Pippa said a little awkwardly that for a man of commerce Uncle Preston had shown excellent farming sense since the Southern Highlands appeared so lush and rich, but he laughed and brushed that aside.

'No real farms here, girl, it's more a showplace. Oh, yes, you'll see fine orchards, prize cows and horses, but mostly it's a retreat for retired country folk who have had their day out west but can't face the confines of the city now they're on in years. It's quite a rich area, in its residents as well as its soil. Social, too.'

Uncle Preston's description tied up with their train companion's account of the district, thought Pippa, though certainly that brown man with his pipe could never be described as social.

Davy was rubbing his cake into crumbs and Pippa could see that Uncle Preston was watching him. Rena would be right, she thought, he would be mean in the little things; that was how he had got on. Her brother was tired, she decided. He needed rest.

She got up, saying she would see to him, and Rena nodded casually . . . then suddenly, at the same time as a car pulled up on the drive, she jumped to her feet, fairly hustled Pippa out, and said, 'No, I will. You go upstairs.'

'But, Rena, I—'

'Daddy, take her.'

'But it's the doctor, Rena,' Uncle Preston objected, looking through the window, 'and it's me he's come to see.' He sounded peeved.

Pippa, looking at him, could well believe he was the reason for the doctor's visit. The chauffeur had said he was not the best, and she had noticed when they had arrived he had a bad colour. Now, away from the sun, that pallor was even more pronounced.

'Glen will see to you *afterwards*, Daddy. Do as I say. Do it now.'

In another minute both Uncle Preston and Pippa were in the hall.

Pippa could hear steps, she could hear a clear, pleasant male voice, then Rena's high smooth voice in gentle response.

'Ho-ho,' said Uncle Preston scornfully . . . he seemed to ho-ho a lot . . . 'now she's put that plum in her mouth, and for all people, *him*. I can't afford him, Pippa. You may think I was joking when I said that before about my present circumstances, about fortunes running out, but I wasn't. She, of course, will never believe it, never having been deprived in all her life. But it's true. Look, Pippa, I'll put you in the picture, this picture my spoiled girl means to paint.'

But Uncle Preston didn't. Not then. His daughter came to the door, and something had happened in the few minutes that had elapsed between their hurried retreat and the doctor's arrival. Rena wore a charming buttercup-hued overall, a nursing-type overall. With her shining golden colouring she looked quite beautiful.

And not just beautiful but dedicated as well. Rena's eyes were soft and docilely downcast. Her smile was sweet.

'Doctor Burt will see you now, Daddy. Take my arm, dear.'

She took it for him and led him back through the door, closing the door definitely before Pippa could glimpse this Doctor Burt.

The mysterious Doctor Burt. Pippa could not help but think that as she climbed the stairs. He must be a very exceptional man to ring that change so soon. One minute a pretty, petulant, headstrong girl, the next minute a tender nurse.

Pippa crossed to the window and looked curiously out, hoping to catch a glimpse of Doctor Burt, but—

She saw the incinerator, the waste-bins and the mulch heap instead.

CHAPTER TWO

PIPPA did not see Doctor Burt in the days that followed, even though he called regularly because Uncle Preston had had another turn.

'What's wrong with your father?' she asked Rena on one of the few occasions she met up with her cousin.

Rena shrugged, if perhaps not actually callously then certainly carelessly. 'Something or other,' she said, and her answer was at a complete variance to her attire, for, as well as the nursing uniform, Rena now had taken to wearing a professional veil whenever the doctor called. She said it was to keep her hair, that gleaming gold hair, away from her face, but it was still a very becoming veil. 'When one grows older things happen,' Rena said vaguely about her parent.

She was not so unkind as simply untouched, Pippa decided. Like Pippa, Rena had no mother, her maternal parent, too, having died early in her life, but *un*like Pippa she had no Aunt Helen. Pippa could find a great pity in her for that. Rena might have a father, but Uncle Preston was entirely a business person, never, Pippa remembered distantly yet with love, like her own father. Preston Franklin had a fatherly regard, but it was mainly a massive paternal pride, pride that Rena was a Franklin after himself.

Pippa thought of Uncle Preston as someone who once he got something into his mind would not let go of it. For instance, his comfortable status (even though he complained about reversals) must have come through long hard application as well as a natural acumen. She felt he had passed that iron determination on to his daughter,

28

and whatever it was ... though that should be *who*ever it was, thought Pippa, for unmistakably it was this Doctor Burt ... she wanted, she would leave nothing undone not to get her own way.

For some reason part of that programme was to have *Pippa* away. Had she not been the owl, the rabbit so long, Pippa might have been complimented over this, but she had no illusions about herself. She was that 'little brown thing' that Rena had described to her father.

So far, apart from not wanting her present, Rena had been quite friendly to Pippa. Having her father to complete her little act whenever Doctor Burt attended, she had had no need yet to deprive Pippa of Davy, for Pippa felt she knew now why the pair of them, Rena's distant English cousins, were here in Tombonda. It was that determination of Rena's, that iron resolve to get what she wanted. Evidently she had tried other methods with the elusive doctor, then recognized the possibility of this one. Shrewdly she had built up a scene for herself ... Uncle Preston had said painted a picture ... and she had had the money to do it, to bring the two of them, though only one really was needed, *Davy*, over from England. She never really had taken to Davy, Pippa knew now. She didn't dislike him, she simply had no feeling about it at all, but he had happened at a right moment, and she had grabbed what offered. Just now she could play the humanitarian role without the little boy, her father could complete a tableau set out for this Doctor Burt, but when Uncle Preston was around again Pippa had no doubt that Davy would take his place, and much more picturesquely, for there was something infinitely winning in the tender caring of a child.

What was he like, this doctor, for Rena to be so keen? So keen even that she did what could have been termed 'homework' on him. She sought out Pippa and asked her advice on nursing.

'I was a typist, Rena.'

'But you've looked after Davy.'

'Never professionally.'

'Only a few things, Pippa, sensible, convincing things will do.'

'Convincing to whom, Rena?'

'It's really nothing to do with you, Pippa. You've been brought over here free and you are enjoying free board, so I hardly think—'

'I didn't mean it like that. I mean what manner of person is to be convinced. If it's someone who understands a nurse's duties—'

'It's Glen Burt,' said Rena quite calmly. A pause. 'I'm marrying him.'

No 'I hope to'. No 'If I do'. Had Uncle Preston been like that when he decided to be a business success?

'Glen is not the usual type,' Rena continued. 'I mean not – well, not like Dom Hardy.' Domrey Hardy shared his overseer duties between the Franklin property on this side of the hill and the Crag property on the other, the Southern Highlands estates not being large enough to warrant an individual man. Pippa had met him and been favourably impressed. He seemed the born all-round farmer, she thought, the right man for a mixed district like this where piggeries, dairy farming, poultry runs and orchards found the weather equally favourable. She felt sure he would have had his own farm had he had the means.

'Dom is transparent, you can see what he's thinking, and that is of me,' Rena said with the lack of pleasure that beautiful *accustomed* girls often show.

'But Glen,' she continued, 'is unaware of me. He is so dedicated, so lit up. It's different to meet a man like that.'

'You've been spoiled, Rena,' Pippa smiled tolerantly. She suddenly found herself thinking of Crag, and wondering how apparent *he* had been. Was that over-apparency the reason he had come back from his 'Big Country' to Tombonda to see what had happened between himself and the girl next door? Had he been too easy for Rena? Would Rena tell him so when he asked her as he had told Pippa on the train that he would: 'What gives?'

She had not seen Crag yet, though Davy had spoken of him persistently and longingly. She had had the idea of walking the little boy over the hill to renew the acquaintance, for Davy had certainly made an idol of him, only she had been forbidden. It was ridiculous, really, and she didn't understand it, but on the first morning that she had visited Uncle Preston in his sickroom, an approved visit since Doctor Burt was not expected until noon, she had said in answer to how she was filling in time a casual, 'Looking around, Uncle Preston. This afternoon I thought I'd take Davy over to the next estate.'

'Crag's?'

'Yes.'

'*No*, my girl.'

'No, Uncle Preston?'

'*No.*'

'But, Uncle Preston—'

'*No*. Do you hear?'

'Yes, I do.' She couldn't see any reason, though, but Uncle Preston was not supposed to talk much, so she had left it at that. Evidently Rena was unconcerned where she went so long as she was not around when Glen Burt was here, but Uncle Preston had been quite emphatic.

'I suppose I have been spoiled,' shrugged Rena, continuing on with her musings. 'I know I'm attractive. And that's what challenges me. He ... Glen ... doesn't notice.'

31

'Do you love him or are you enjoying the challenge?' Pippa dared.

'They're both the same when you've been bored like I have.'

'Oh, Rena—' began Pippa, but Rena broke in irritably:

'Give me some nursing hints.'

'I only took an aide course,' demurred Pippa, but as Rena stuck out a stubborn lip she complied.

'A nurse needs to be adaptable, tactful and discreet. Her patient is her first concern.'

'Something more concrete. I could pretend all that.'

Pippa told her about room temperature, the storing of medicines, the necessity for a stock of good temper and patience, the need to concede yet stand firm.

'Something definite,' Rena demanded.

'I've only dealt with children, with Davy.'

'That's what I want, because Father will be up again very soon, and I'll have to use your brother. Oh, don't look like that. I wish him the best as you do, but if I can avail myself at the same time, I will. *Tell* me something, Pippa.'

'It's as well to be able to amuse a sick child,' Pippa said leadenly. Why had she ever come here? she wondered.

Rena must have seen she had gone a little too far. 'Tell me about Davy,' she asked quite gently. 'What exactly is it?'

'An incurable circulatory disease. That is, incurable now.'

'You mean something might be found?'

'I tell myself so, and no one really can say definitely these days, but—' Pippa looked away.

'All this will interest Glen.' Rena became brisk again. 'He wants to do research. That costs money, and you'd think he'd be aware that I could help him.' She looked around at her affluent home with satisfaction. 'Tombonda,' she went on, 'is only till Glen goes to Europe, or America, or – or somewhere *right away*.' She said the last almost with passionate fervour, and Pippa looked at her in puzzlement. 'Right away,' her cousin repeated.

Pippa thought of how she had declared that love and challenge were the same when you were bored and she wondered had the doctor been any other man who had not thrown his heart at Rena's feet would any other men be as attractive to her cousin? Undoubtedly, her thoughts ran on, Crag Crag's failure with Rena had been his over-susceptibility. Perhaps if she saw the brown man before he returned to his Big Country, to his Yantumara, Falling Star, she could put him wise. A pity for such a family-anxious person to waste 'time for living life as it should be lived' by making wrong moves.

That afternoon Pippa saw Glen Burt. She was gathering flowers to brighten her room when his car pulled up. She got behind a shrub, knowing that Rena would be angry if she was around, but she had a good look at him.

She liked him instantly, and she would have loved to have talked to him about Davy. There was a gentleness yet a strength to him, she thought. No wonder that Rena . . .

Rena sought her out later and said quite frankly: 'Father's to be up and around again quite soon, indeed, he'll be allowed on the patio tomorrow, so I'll be using your brother. I'm not asking "Any objection?" because even if you had one, like Dom always has objections, I wouldn't listen.'

She always brought Domrey Hardy into it, Pippa mused. She answered her cousin: 'That's all right, Rena, so long as Davy has attention.'

33

'He's going to have heaps of it,' Rena assured her.

Uncle Preston was out on the patio the next day as promised, and during the morning he had a word with Pippa.

'You've stopped away from next door as I said?'

'Why, yes, Uncle Preston.'

'You're entitled to a reason.'

'I think I am. You see, I met Mr. Crag on the train coming down to Tombonda, and Davy has been asking about him.'

'Then Rena can take him over.'

'I think,' Pippa said clearly, 'that that might be suitable, for Mr. Crag said on the journey that he wanted an understanding with Rena.' Actually he had said he wanted to know 'What gives?' but he had meant an understanding.

She waited for Uncle Preston to explain, and, always the business man, he did.

'They had a semi-agreement,' he grunted. 'It was just after Rena had that fall off Bunting, I remember.' – Bunting was one of the ponies – 'I thought everything was set between the pair of them, and I was pleased, even though ...' Uncle Preston was silent for a moment. 'Yes, I was pleased,' he took up again, 'because Crag could keep my girl in the way she was accustomed.

'Then that fellow, that doctor fellow joined the act,' he went on. He glowered.

'And Rena fell in love with him?'

'I don't know about this love,' grumbled Uncle Preston testily.

'You must do. You married Aunt Millicent.'

'She was suitable,' he replied. – That was typical of Uncle Preston, and Pippa half-smiled.

'You don't find Doctor Burt suitable?' she asked.

'He's a dreamer. You only have to look at him.'

34

'I haven't,' admitted Pippa. Well, actually she hadn't, only between the boughs of a shrub.

'Then you will,' he promised.

'Rena doesn't want that, though I don't know why.'

'Don't fish for compliments. You're pretty, Pippa. Not a beauty like my girl, but lots of men like a quiet type like you. She doesn't want you because she's afraid Glen might be one of those men. Which would suit me. Oh, yes, you'll meet Burt, my girl.'

Uneasily Pippa had left Uncle Preston. At no time had she expected to be rapturously happy in Australia, so long as Davy was contented had been all she had asked, but this in-between position in which she found herself, in between Rena and her father, was certainly something she had *not* anticipated.

That she had not dreamed up the situation was established at once by Rena meeting her in the hall just beyond the patio.

'I know what he said,' Rena pounced at once.

'It was unimportant, Rena.'

'Not unimportant to me. I told you I was going to marry Glen.'

'Yes, I heard you, but I can't see where I come in.'

Rena looked hard at her but did not explain. 'I meant it, Pippa. *I* am marrying Glen. So I don't want you in this.'

'I don't want to be in it, either, I just want a quiet life with Davy.'

'Then you've come to the wrong place if you interfere. Father doesn't want Glen for me, so he's encouraging you to step in. But I won't have it, Pippa. Do you understand?'

Pippa said, confused, 'He's forbidden me to take Davy over to Crag's.'

Rena shrugged carelessly at that and the shrug

prompted Pippa to complain: '*You* tell me to keep away from the doctor, yet your *father* tells me to keep away from your neighbour. What am I to do?'

'What I say, of course.'

'And that is to—'

'To see Crag. To do what you like with Crag. I don't want him.' A toss of the golden head.

About to add, 'Neither do I', Pippa said impulsively instead, 'But you did once.'

'I don't know if I did,' Rena shrugged again. 'I think it was just – just—' But she did not finish it. She set her lips instead.

Pippa broke the little silence that followed by repeating, 'You must appreciate my position, Rena. Your father forbids me to see Mr. Crag. You forbid me to see Doctor Burt. I have no particular desire to see either, so what gives?'

What gives? Crag Crag's drawled words. She thought of Davy's Big Country man and wondered why she had copied the foolish phrase.

'Oh, just make do with Dom,' advised Rena crossly, for the overseer was coming up the drive now. Quite rudely the girl turned and left Pippa to greet the young farmer alone. Dom took it philosophically. 'Always,' he sighed, 'Rena is running away from me. It was just a buying authority I needed. Something dull to do with pigs.'

'Only *you* don't find it dull?' deduced Pippa sympathetically.

'No,' he admitted, 'I love what I'm doing.'

'Except that you'd sooner be doing it for yourself?'

'And with—' he began impulsively. Then he stopped.

It came to Pippa that if anyone could help her in her odd position, the in-between uncertainty in which she found herself, in between stubborn Uncle Preston and determined Rena, it could be this kind young man.

'Mr. Hardy—' she ventured.

'Can't it be Dom?' he smiled. 'Admittedly we're not the wide untrammelled west—'

'The big country.'

'Yes, but even in these Southern Highlands formality is out of place.'

'I'm Pippa,' she agreed warmly, for she couldn't help liking him. As he nodded back, she began again, 'Dom—'

But she wasn't to ask his advice or help or information, because Rena's imperative voice called to her through a window.

'Where's Davy?' Rena asked sharply.

With a little gesture to Domrey Hardy, Pippa went inside. Rena met her as she came through the door.

'Glen is coming at once to give Father a final look-over before he's allowed right out of the house and around the grounds again. Daddy's obviously thriving, so no doubt Glen will make this a last visit unless he's called out especially. But he's one of those righteous doctors you can't call. I mean he wants to know if it's absolutely necessary.' A little rueful laugh. 'What a man! So I thought I'd present Davy today, start a new programme of events. But the wretched boy is missing.'

'Davy isn't here!' Pippa said urgently.

'Oh, don't take on, Pippa, he can't have gone far. The trouble is where? Glen will be out in half an hour.'

Pippa turned on her furiously. 'I don't care when he comes out, Rena, all I care is that Davy is missing. Have you looked in his room?'

'And your room and every other room. The garden. The orchard. I even went down to the chicken run. That deplorable boy—'

'He could have gone into the planting.' Like most of the estates in the Highlands area, the Franklin property

37

included a small afforestation section where softwood was being raised. Though it was called the planting, the trees had been in for some years, and were fairly well advanced, mostly pine, already spreading their branches to meet and form a concealing green tent. Pippa had walked through once and nearly lost herself among the identical trees. If Davy had ventured in—

Brushing past Rena, Pippa ran out of the room, then out of the house, down past the cultivation, the stables, the piggery, orchard, the resting paddocks.

'Davy,' she called, 'Davy!'

She was aware that in parkland like this there was little fear of the boy being lost, that Rena was probably right when she had contemptuously dismissed, 'Oh, don't take on, he can't have gone far.' But even in a little distance the strain could be too much for her brother in his delicate state. Also, if he had ventured into the planting ... the forest, he called it ... he could have panicked when he found himself, as Pippa had, walking round in circles, and, being a child, not had the sense to know that in such a small afforestation it was not far to the open fields again.

Reaching the deep green and plunging into it, Pippa called once more, 'Davy! Davy! It's Pippa, Davy. Stand quite still then shout out my name, darling.' She waited, but there was no answer.

She combed the woods thoroughly. At any other time she would have rejoiced in the cool pine tang of the needles brushing her face, the soft carpet of the fallen ones beneath her feet, but not now.

Stumbling over roots she kept up her searching and calling, then found she was climbing a small rise. At the bottom of the rise a little stream purled by, and now she found a new fear. She ran forward and was relieved to see that the brook was quite shallow, but often deep pools formed at intervals, she knew, and she looked nervously up and down stream, wondering which way to search.

Then to her surprise she saw a patch through the trees. She must be out of the planting, but on the other side to Franklin's. Crag Crag's side. Sobbing a little in relief, she ran forward, past more tilled ground, some of it under cultivation, then at last she saw the house, not elegantly two-storeyed like Uncle Preston's but leisurely and spreading. The sort of a house you expected from a big countryman. Strictly Western-style.

Snatching a breath, she began to run again, but already she had run too fast for too long, and a sharp pain halted her. She refused to accept the pain and pushed herself forward once more, her heart pumping so acutely in its effort to cope that at last she was forced to stop definitely, not only stop but sink to the ground.

When Crag joined her a moment afterward, he just left her like that, wisely waiting for her to recover, checking Davy, who was by his side, that he did the same.

Davy's scolding, 'You naughty girl to run like that, you always tell me not to' were the sweetest words Pippa felt she had ever heard. She knew she was going to cry, and that was something she never did in front of Davy, but how to stop the relieved tears?

Then she found she could cry in safety, for the brown man was telling Davy to come and see something, and they were both gone. By the time they returned, her breath had returned, and her eyes were dry. Davy forgot about his admonishment in the excitement of whatever it was the man had shown him, but Crag Crag found time to say as they followed Davy, who was leading the way triumphantly to the Crag house: 'He's right, you know, you were a naughty girl. Why?'

'I thought you understood the position,' she said stiffly,

and she nodded briefly to her brother. 'I told you in the train—'

'Oh, that.' He gave a hunch of his great shoulders. 'But you were worrying for yourself, not for the scrubber. What good could that do?'

'It was Davy concerning me, of course,' she defended. 'He could have got lost in the planting and worked himself up to a pitch which could be dangerous. Then there's a stream and—'

She stopped. Stopped her progress as well as her answer to him, for he had paused to pack his eternal pipe, and halted her with him. She felt infuriated with him for his calmness, for his deliberation. Except that Davy now was too far ahead she would have grabbed her brother's hand and returned him at once and without any more explanation to Uplands.

'Look,' said Crag Crag, still doing his packing and tapping thing with the tobacco, 'you shouldn't have run like that, it did nobody any good. It did Davy no good ... you worrying over him never does any good. Children live in the present, not the past nor the future. They're such little scrubbers they have nothing in the past to regret and nothing in the future to fear, so they're content.

'Then' ... giving her no chance to edge in ... 'it did you no good. You're still out of breath.

'Then' ... lighting the pipe he had been busy on ... 'it did me no good.' His match made a little scratching sound.

'I fail to see where you come into it.'

'Shall I tell you, then?' He had started walking once more, had taken her along with him, but now he stopped again. Stopped abruptly.

'No,' she said hurriedly, not knowing why her heart was keeping up its thumping so long. 'No, it doesn't matter. I'm sorry I was so foolish, and I do see your point.

It would have put you out had I collapsed in your grounds.'

He did not comment on that at once. He looked her burningly up and down, then he said deliberately: 'When I was at school we used to call kids like you stinkers. You know damn well I wasn't thinking of that.'

Now was her turn to ask, 'What, then?' but Pippa blurted instead, 'Davy has reached your house.'

She saw that the house was named briefly (and rather clownishly, she considered) simply: 'Ku'.

'Meaning shelter,' the brown man said, guessing her scorn. 'That's what it is for me. *Home* is up north, at Falling Star.'

'Rather elaborate for a mere shelter,' she remarked. 'Oh, naughty Davy, he's gone in.'

'He was there before, so why not now? It was the scrubber who saw you running out of the planting.' They had reached the wide verandah by this, and he stood aside and nodded for Pippa to climb shallow steps into a long cool hall.

'It's not like Uncle Preston's,' Pippa murmured, for she could think of nothing else just then to say.

'It's the same as the big country house. Big country men only know one style – long halls, rooms each side, verandahs all round like the brim of a hat. Makes for coolness, only coolness isn't needed much here, not in the Southern Highlands.' He laughed. 'But it didn't matter to my father, for being a big country man he naturally put in chimneys everywhere. They all go out and up. It's not what you'd call perfect planning building a cool house and having to make it warm, but I'm glad he built big country style, I like the look of a fire.'

'So do I,' chirruped Davy from the fireside of the room into which Crag had led Pippa, 'especially when you make toast.'

'Davy,' reprimanded Pippa, 'you shouldn't have run away like this. Why did you?'

'I didn't want to see another doctor. I'm always seeing doctors. So I thought I'd ask Crag. But Crag's been telling me about Manager and how he had this bad leg.'

'Your Falling Star manager?' asked Pippa politely, and Davy went into peals of laughter.

'No, he's a bay, and so is Major, but Captain is grey, and Taffy is—'

'Get back to Manager,' said Crag.

'Well, Manager had to see the vet. Then he had to see him again. And again.' A big breath. 'Then again. But in the end—'

'In the end?' Pippa's throat was dry.

'He won a hurdle. They have these races up in the big country, you know. Real jockeys and pretend jockeys . . . I mean not jockeys who are jockeys all the time. The real jockeys wear silks, but the others wear overalls or jeans or crash helmets even. So Manager won by not missing out on the vet. And I'll do the same, Pippa, because Crag says—'

Crag says. Crag says. The little voice went on and on, not giving Pippa a chance to insert, 'Yes, dear, but now we have to go home.'

At length she did, though. She said accusingly to Davy: '*Your* vet is at Uplands right this minute and you're not there to be checked, so you'll never win a hurdle.'

'Reckon he will from now on, though, eh, scrubber?' drawled Crag. 'Reckon he'll remember Manager.' He looked narrowly at Pippa, asking: 'Is this vet one Glen Burt?'

'Yes.'

'Then I reckon I needn't drive you back. I reckon Rena will be scorching up the drive any minute now.' A short knowing laugh.

Davy's attention was on a racing manual Crag had handed him, so there was no need to talk carefully. Pippa knew that when Davy read he read with all of him, everything else was excluded.

'I expect she will,' she agreed. 'She plans to use Davy.'

'You don't object?'

'Not so long as my brother has attention.'

'What about you?'

'What do you mean?'

'You don't want attention yourself? This doctor's attention? You see, I've met Burt.'

'I haven't.' Her colour was high.

'Then when you do you mightn't like the way Rena has things worked out.'

'Oh, really—'

'Yes, really. He's an exceptional fellow. Handsome, too. You mightn't like sitting back while Rena does a maternal act in flowing veil and what-have-you to spring a trap that could have been yours.'

'Actually you mean *you* don't like it,' she said angrily. 'Not from Rena.'

'Me?' He was patently surprised.

'Oh, don't give me that,' flung Pippa. 'You said yourself in the train that you had to see Rena to find out what gives.'

'Remember what I say, don't you,' he said, absurdly pleased, or anyway, Pippa found it absurd.

'Also,' she continued coldly, 'Uncle Preston told me of your semi-agreement with Rena.'

'Not semi on his part,' grinned Crag. 'Old Preston was all for it. That is' . . . thoughtfully . . . 'failing—'

He did not finish, and Pippa said as she had before: 'Really.'

43

'Don't repeat that any more,' appealed Crag. He waited, then: 'Look, Pippa' ... *Pippa*, Pippa revolted ... 'I'll put you straight. There *was* a semi-agreement. I'm sick of being a bachelor, and I don't mind admitting it.'

'Time running out and all that?' caustically.

'Exactly. But I still wasn't so keen that I would have rushed into it. As it happened I didn't need to. *I* was the rushed one.'

'That's very ungallant. It's also untrue.'

'It's not ungallant. Rena Franklin ran after me like you just ran after the scrubber. Oh, I was flattered all right. Just down from the bush and a girl storms me. A beautiful one. Only—' A quiet smile.

'It's not true,' interrupted Pippa. 'You rushed Rena, and she got sick of it. Everyone rushes her, except Glen Burt, and that's why—'

'You believe that?' He looked at her incredulously.

'Why not?'

'You wouldn't think of believing that she's running away instead?'

'You just said she ran after you.'

'Yes, but she didn't mean to catch up. Oh, no, not our Rena.'

'I simply can't follow you,' Pippa said after a little pause. 'It's all so contradictory. You said she rushed you, then you say she was running away. It makes no sense. But I do advise you' ... briskly now ... 'to – to court Rena differently. Don't be so – so susceptible. *Then* you might win.'

'And you think that's what I want?'

'You have said so, haven't you? You spoke about that design of man and woman' ... her cheeks flushed ... 'and how it has to have its start.'

'Reckon I did say that,' he nodded, 'only I was forgetting something else, something the old man once told me.'

'Uncle Preston?'

'My old man. My dad. His life and my mother's life together was the only kind I wanted.' He took up his pipe, 'I asked Dad once how – well, how you *knew*.' He turned the pipe over in his big hand. For Crag Crag, Pippa thought, he actually looked shy.

'Yes?' she asked gently, wondering at her gentleness.

'He said . . . my father said it was a thousand candles.'

'All lit up?' Davy was looking up from the horse book now.

'All lit together, scrubber. Reckon I forgot it for a while, but do you know what' . . . he was lighting the pipe now . . . 'I've remembered it again.'

'Absence doesn't always make the heart grow fonder,' nodded Pippa crisply, 'now that you're near to Rena again you've remembered it.'

'Rena?' If she hadn't been worried how Rena was going to react to Davy's absence and not reacting properly herself, Pippa would have said there was a negation in his voice.

'Here she is now,' advised Davy, peering out of the window. He added wickedly, 'Purple with rage.'

Rena certainly looked angry, thought Pippa, joining Davy, she was flushed and actually tousled. She put her arm protectively around her brother.

'She spits, but so far she doesn't bite,' advised Crag calmly from his side of the room. 'I had a wild cat like that once at Falling Star.'

'Did you, Crag?' came in Davy eagerly. 'Tell me about it.'

'Later, scrubber. You take your sister out to the kitchen and help her make a pot of tea. I'm going to spread oil.'

Out in the large galley ... big country style again in its capaciousness, in its large centre table ... Davy said, 'I didn't see any oil. I wonder if he's spreading it now.'

'Yes,' contributed Pippa, 'I wonder.'

But by the quietness in the room they had just left, in spite of Crag Crag's refusal of Rena, Pippa had more an impression of candles. A thousand candles as two people looked across a space at each other.

All lit together.

CHAPTER THREE

On their way back to Uplands, Pippa was relieved to find
her cousin almost mellow. After Rena's angry expression
as she left her car on the drive to storm into Crag's Ku . . .
purple with rage, Davy had said . . . she had trembled for
her brother. Davy had literally never known an admonishing word, not a seriously admonishing one, all his small
life, and the words Rena had seemed about to throw at
him had raised all sorts of fears for that sensitive little
boy. But either the tea she had brought in or the oil Crag
had spread . . . Davy was still puzzling over that oil . . .
had done something. Rena now was quite relaxed.

'It's always the way with Crag,' Rena said quite am-
iably, negotiating a bend, 'he calms me down. Actually
we two would make good chemistry.'

It seemed an unromantic way to put it, Pippa thought,
she preferred candlelight, but she supposed it came to the
same thing. Rena's happy mood also meant no scolding
for Davy, and for that she should be pleased, and she was,
of course, except . . . well, except . . . Her lips moved unconsciously. She was not aware she spoke.

'Pippa,' came in Davy from the back seat, 'why did you
just say candlelight twice? It's daytime, and anyway,
there's 'lectric here at Tombonda.'

'Yes, darling.'

'And 'lectric, too, up at Falling Star. They have plant,
Crag told me. It's not like a plant in the ground, it's a
machine plant, Crag told me.'

'Yes, darling,' Pippa said mechanically. She was
pleased there was no reckoning from Rena, but somehow
she still felt oddly heavy.

47

'Our Davy,' Rena was saying cheerfully, 'wasn't needed after all. Glen spent a long time on Father.'

'How is he?'

'Oh, quite all right, I should say,' vaguely. 'After Glen finished the examination I got our doctor on to the topic of Davy, and succeeded in interesting him enough to come out if . . . when . . . he's asked. I'm sure of it.'

'Doesn't a doctor always do things like that?'

'I told you before, Pippa, Glen is the frightfully dedicated type. He wouldn't come just for a fee, there'd have to be a proper reason. I told him what you told me about Davy – that circulatory thing. He was certainly keen. I should say he'll come whenever I ring.'

'Thank you.' Pippa's voice was dry.

'The trouble is,' Rena continued, self-absorbed as usual, 'he'll have to meet you, and you know how I feel about that.'

'I don't know why.'

'Oh, come off it,' said Rena slangily, 'you must look in the mirror sometimes. You're pretty, Pippa, something I never expected, otherwise I wouldn't have had you here. Surely someone somewhere at some time must have told you that.'

'No one did.'

'It takes some believing.'

'Then you'll just have to believe.'

'You mean you've reached the age of twenty . . . you'd be that, Pippa, you were some years junior to me . . . and no man has told you!'

'None.'

'It takes some believing,' Rena said again.

'It's true. I haven't met anyone. My life has been taken up with—' Pippa gave a brief indicative nod of her head.

'A child can't take up that much.'

48

'*Love* can.'

'Then preserve me from it!'

'But you already have it, haven't you? Or is it – challenge? Oh, I'm sorry, Rena, I'm speaking out of turn.'

'You are,' said Rena, 'but after all I started this. Frankly, Pippa, I don't know much about – well, about what you just said, I – I mean—'

'You mean love?'

'Yes. You see ... well ...' Suddenly and unnecessarily Rena put her foot down on the accelerator and the car fairly leapt ahead, Davy, taken unawares, tumbling forward. Pippa caught him before any damage was done. Rena tossed, 'Sorry.' As Pippa righted Davy again she saw that Rena wore an oddly pinched look.

To bridge an awkward silence Pippa asked, 'What am I to say to Uncle Preston if he questions me? He was very adamant that I didn't go over to Crag's.'

'I doubt if he'll ask you now he's allowed outdoors again. My father is primarily a business man and he'll be so anxious to check up whether Dom Hardy is still ministering his estate as it should be, that he hasn't been giving more time to Ku than to Uplands, that he'll probably forget all about it. That's typical of Daddy. Pennies first. Which reminds me, *you* can be of use to our overseer, Pippa. Father will like that. So will I. At least it will keep you from Glen.'

'Rena, I told you I have no wish to know this Doctor Burt.'

'What about his knowing you?'

'I can't help that, and I'm sorry. If I could help it I'd—'

'Yes, I suppose so. But he'll certainly want you for data on Davy. Apart from giving it to him, Pippa, just don't linger, will you? Just – just watch it.'

It seemed incredible to Pippa that Rena's lovely red

mouth could form these slangy threats. Only that somewhere somehow they rang false, she could have felt angry
with her cousin.

'How can I help Dom Hardy?' she asked instead.

'The Southern Highlands comprise the perfect stud for
pigs, cows, horses,' shrugged Rena, 'and blessed events
always call for help. If you consult Dom Hardy's official
calendar you'll see quite a birth list ticked up.' She
paused. 'Also, can you ride?'

'How well would I be required to?'

'He'll tell you.' Again the shrug. — What an odd girl she
was, hard, yet somehow defiantly, determinedly so. It
puzzled Pippa.

When they reached the house Uncle Preston was out
walking round the different sections, as his daughter had
said he would, and when Pippa joined him he did not
question her about Ku. Instead he kept up a grumble
about his monetary affairs, the same grumble Pippa had
heard before, mostly concerning his daughter and her
blithe refusal to realize their present position.

She took the old man's hand to help him over some
uneven ground, noticing how thin it had become during
his illness. 'Down to your last million, Uncle,' she
teased.

'You can laugh,' he retorted, 'but I'm genuinely concerned. For some time now the market in which I'm vit-
ally involved has been ... But what's the use of telling
you?'

'Often telling helps.' But Pippa said it without much
feeling. Always she had been poor, really poor, and looking around this beautiful estate she had to smile wryly at
Uncle Preston's idea of straitened circumstances.

The old man continued his grumbling. 'How could
Rena face up to it?' he said.

'But this place alone—'

'Wouldn't keep her in shoes. Rena has been used to everything, *everything*. That was why I was resigned about Crag for her after ... well, once I knew, once I could see that—' As he had previously, Pippa recalled, Uncle Preston did not finish his thought. Returning to Crag again, he sighed regretfully: 'There's money there.'

'Rena-money,' smiled Pippa, and her uncle nodded.

'I thought that least she would be right that way, then what does that minx do but play up again.'

'The doctor?'

'Yes.'

'No doubt you've spoiled her, Uncle.'

'No doubt,' he admitted ruefully. 'I wasn't a young parent and she was an exceptionally beautiful girl. Yes, I spoiled her, Pippa. Still, it's only recently she's been like this. Always capricious, of course, but not like this. She used to lead me a merry dance, that was my Rena, but sometimes I think it was only after her fall off Bunting ...'

He had said something about this before, Pippa remembered. She asked: 'Was she hurt?'

'Never Rena, she's a perfect horsewoman, even handles falls.' He chuckled.

There was a silence, and Pippa broke it with the information that Rena had suggested that she help the overseer with the Uplands estate. As Rena had said, her father was pleased.

'Yes,' he nodded practically, 'there's enough idle hands at Uplands. Though I've no doubt that that wasn't her reason, not Rena's, she just wanted you out of the way when the doctor fellow calls.'

'I have to see Doctor Burt some time, he'll want information about Davy.'

'Then you'd better look your worst,' ho-ho'd Uncle Preston.

Feeling uncomfortable at the turn of the conversation, Pippa said there was no time like the present to offer her services to the overseer. She helped Uncle Preston to the patio, touched by his exhaustion after such a small expedition, then went to the back of the house and across the lawn to the stables.

Domrey Hardy was sitting in his office absorbed in estate affairs when she entered, but he looked up and smiled and cleared a chair for her.

She told him that it had been suggested that she help him.

'Mr. Franklin back on the job again,' he nodded.

'No, actually it was Rena who told me, but Uncle Preston was quite pleased.'

'Yes. Rena.' Dom looked down at his papers again.

A silence grew. Pippa broke it at length by saying briskly: 'I believe you have a string of happy events, Dom.'

'That's right.' Dom came out of his absorption and was the alert overseer again. 'Candytuft foals in a month. The piggery will be a nursery in several weeks. As for Velvet—'

'With a name like that Velvet must be the cow.'

'Yes, and she's predictably unpredictable in her timing. She could be right this minute, next week, next month. No official forty weeks for our girl, she shortens or lengthens the period to her own liking.'

'Doesn't a bull calf generally take longer?'

'Yes. But I sometimes think rules were made to be broken by our Velvet. Also, going on previous confinements, she's touchy. We have, of course, a good vet, but Velvet usually chooses a moment when a vet isn't available.'

'I might be able to help.'

'The idea is attractive, but have you helped before?'

'I lived in a country village and at least I was aware,' Pippa replied.

She next brought up the subject of riding. 'Rena said I might be of use there, and that you'd let me know.'

Dom had put the pen he had been doodling with back on the stand and he folded his arms on the desk. He was looking across at Pippa yet not looking at her somehow. 'Determined, isn't she?' he said quietly.

'What, Dom?'

'You're not to upstage her. That's it, isn't it. – Oh, I'm sorry, Pippa, I'm talking rot.' He tried to brush it aside, but Pippa persisted.

'What is it, Dom?' she asked again.

When he did not reply, she said: 'It's Rena, isn't it?'

'Yes.'

'What did you mean by upstage?' – Crag had said almost the same thing, she recalled, only he had expressed it: 'Springing a trap that could have been yours.'

Wretchedly Dom said: 'She's determined not to have you around when Burt's around, which means she's determined on him, and when Rena's determined . . .' He said it almost unemotionally, but Pippa saw that his knuckles in the big capable farmer hands were white from the tightness of his clenched fists.

At once he said again, 'Sorry, Pippa. Sheer rot. Of course I can do with you. How well do you ride?'

'How well is required?' She had asked that of Rena and Rena had said that Dom Hardy would explain.

'The Southern Highlands is the home of the pony clubs,' he told her. 'With a moderately bracing climate like we enjoy, how could it not be the perfect place? So we train for shows, for all the equestrian gatherings. We try to impart the usual accomplishments . . . canters, trots, even dressage.'

'Uplands' horses?'

'No, we accept outside pupils and train them for their owners. This, incidentally, is strictly my own business, Pippa, I pay Mr. Franklin for the exercise space and the stabling.'

'But he seemed pleased I could help you.'

'Well, some of the income goes back to him, so although it's my part of the concern it's to his advantage for it to prosper.'

She nodded, then remarked, 'Uncle Preston says he's in a bad financial position.'

Dom gave a short laugh at that and said nothing. He took Pippa out to a pretty cream pony which he said he was training for a client for the next Royal Show.

'Rickaby needs exercise around your weight, Pippa. Care to try him?'

'I haven't any gear, not even a pair of slacks.' She had brought none. They had not seemed necessary.

'That's all right, there's plenty in the change room.' He nodded back to the stables.

As he saddled the pony, Pippa returned to the stables, found the change room and changed. The clothes that were hung there were all very good. Rena's? And had Rena ridden since her fall from Bunting?

She asked Dom this when she came back again. He was bent over the pony, but he straightened at once. 'Did Rena tell you about that?'

'No. Her father mentioned that she had had a fall.' Pippa did not add that Uncle Preston had complained that his daughter had not been the same since. Instead she said, 'These must be her clothes. They're good.'

'Then if they're good they would be hers,' he said abruptly. He came round to leg Pippa up. His face was unrevealing – intentionally so, Pippa thought.

54

It was a puzzling situation, but once she was on the pony's back she forgot the puzzle. She always had loved riding, and in the village where they had lived it had not been such an expensive pleasure. Though ... smiling ... she had never ridden in a kit as well tailored as this.

She trotted round for a while, then, encouraged by the fact that months out of a saddle had not lessened her ability, she ventured down a track leading from the circle that Dom had flattened out from other exercising. What happened next was entirely her own fault. She should have realized that a 'boarder' here simply to learn the tricks, not present just for the fun of it and certainly not for exploration, would not comprehend the uneven ground as the track petered suddenly out, the bushes began to encroach, the trees crowd in, a dividing fence imprison. The gully creek was her final undoing. Ordinarily it would have been a charming spot, Pippa thought briefly, a place where tranquillity would be the keynote, no sound except the chirping of crickets, the song of a bird, the tinkle of the brook, but it was new and strange to the cream pony, and like all highly bred animals he was over-sensitive to unaccustomed things. Perhaps he saw a shape in the shadows that Pippa could not see, something that frightened him, for, rearing up, he turned and streaked, quite out of control now, away from the shadowy gully. Unfortunately the path the pony took was right beside the boundary fence. Several times Pippa brushed it quite roughly. She thought ruefully that Rena's expensive gear would suffer. But at least, she thought, too, it was better that than the pony.

Now the animal was fairly flying, and though she had always enjoyed a brisk gallop, Pippa had never been good enough to cope with anything like this. She gave up trying to check Rickaby, show him who called the tune, her only thought now was to hold on. Hold on. Hold on, she said desperately as the pony fairly flew over the ground.

She could hear hooves digging in; she would not have thought the little light fellow could have made such a din. Then she saw something streak past her, a second horse, a much larger mount than her own, which would account for that noise. But she had no time to look properly, she was too concerned with her own inability to deal with the racing cream, too aware of the fellow's knowledge, as horses always have such knowledge, that she had lost her touch.

'Pull in!' the voice called authoritatively. Even in her despair she recognized the voice as Crag Crag's, and she called back pleadingly, 'I can't!'

'Then hold on. I'm coming. And when I say Clear, clear your feet from the stirrups. But hang on, Pippa, he'll rear.'

She obeyed mechanically, held on mechanically, freed herself when he called out as he turned his own mount and doubled back to reach over and grab her rein. As he shouted 'Clear!' the cream fellow rose on his hind legs and Pippa felt herself slipping, but her feet at least were free and she was able to be lifted out of the saddle and deposited in front of Crag, then, a few moments later, dropped to the ground.

'Reckon,' said a slow voice, 'you'll have to do better than that when you ride after a scrubber up at Falling Star.' Crag Crag took out his pipe and began his packing act.

His unshakeable calmness usually irritated her, but now it gave her the time she needed to catch her breath. She did not pick him up over his assumption that she would be going to Falling Star, she was too grateful she had not fallen herself. She found a log and sat on it while he secured Rickaby.

'Damn silly thing to do,' he said, when he came back again, 'these are strictly ring ponies, not ring-bark.'

'Ring-bark?'

'Well, you've nearly done that to yourself.' He was looking at the jodhpurs that had received the impact of the boundary fence. They were torn, frayed and rubbed.

'Rena's,' she said forlornly.

'But the skin underneath is yours. Best you give it some attention, girl.'

'I'm all right.'

'If you are it's more than you deserve to be. You should know these fellows are only spit and polish boys, not like—'

'I know, not like the ones who carry you full gallop to flick a scrubber down and pin it by its tail.'

'You remember!' he said with delight.

'Oh, you – you fool!' Pippa replied. She got up and brushed herself. 'I must get back. Dom will wonder where I am.' It occurred to her that she must seem very churlish seeing that but for this man she might not be returning at all, so she added humbly, 'I thank you very much.'

'That's all right.' He grinned. 'I was only thinking of the Franklins. It puts people out to have someone collapse on their grounds.'

'*You* remember.' It was Pippa's turn. They both began to laugh.

'Well,' said Crag, 'that's better than crying, anyway. You better get up as you said. But soak in the bath to-night. Nothing like heat for a graze. Have you anything to apply?'

'The clothes got the impact.'

'You'll find you got impact, too, beneath those clothes. Have the doctor look you over. No.' A brief grin. 'It's Burt, isn't it, so that would be out because of Rena. But see to yourself all the same.'

'I will, and thank you again. By the way, how was it you were here to rescue me?'

'You were rescued, isn't that enough?'

'Do you make a habit of going down gullies in case maidens come along on runaway horses, Mr. Crag?'

'No, Miss Bromley' . . . he knew her name! . . . 'but I do go along the fences at times. It's a bad habit I got into at Falling Star, where it's deadly important.'

'Why?'

'Dingoes.'

'But are there sheep at Falling Star?' At least she knew that dingoes must be kept from sheep.

'No, but it's important that I keep the dingoes on my side for the southerners who do have sheep.'

'That's considerate of you.'

'I've plenty of consideration. Could you do with some?' He was tapping the tobacco down now, and something about that deliberate finger made Pippa feel uncomfortable.

'I'd better go.'

'I'm not stopping you,' he grinned.

'Certainly you're not.'

'I wouldn't be too certain,' he proffered, and his laugh followed her as she grabbed Rickaby's rein and led him back up the hill. What a man! she thought, as she had thought before.

Dom was not around. She was grateful for that, and unsaddled Rickaby at once and rubbed him down. In the change room she examined the jodhpurs and found them frayed and worn but still fit for use. However, she would have to tell Rena. As for herself, the skin was rubbed, as Crag had said, and she had no doubt she would tingle when she got into the hot bath he had advised, but she had come off fairly well.

58

As soon as she got to the house she sought out Rena and apologized about the riding kit.

'It doesn't matter, it was only old stuff I left there. You said you fell?' Rena's eyes were oddly narrowed.

'Yes. My own fault. I shouldn't have taken Rickaby down the gully.'

'Then you weren't with Dom Hardy when it happened?'

'No.'

'No one to pick you up?'

'Yes. Mr. Crag happened to be examining the fence.'

'And he picked you up?'

Something in Rena's voice brought Pippa's eyes flicking up to the girl's blue eyes. They were beautiful eyes, large, heavily-lashed ... and just now bright with tears. Tears? Rena in tears?

But the next minute Pippa told herself she must have imagined it.

'You want to be careful,' Rena said flippantly, 'when you fall. Sometimes it's not just the ground that's hard.'

'What do you mean, Rena?'

'Sometimes it's ...' But Rena did not finish. She simply turned and left.

Pippa staring after her thought that as well as being lovely, Rena could be a very strange girl.

All that week Pippa helped Dom. No blessed events occurred, but there was plenty to do in the stables. Dom had six 'pupils' to learn the niceties of show business. How to canter winningly, come to a gentle halt; remain quiet and erect while a judge circled you.

It was fascinating work, and now that she had learned her lesson not to explore with these strictly arena creatures, Pippa got on quite well.

One afternoon Dom brought an intended rider along

with the 'pupil'. Marilyn was the daughter of a couple who had bought a house in the neighbouring Highlands town of Bilgong, and it was expected that Southern Highlands children ride. Marilyn had lived in a city flat and never ridden, and she looked with frank dislike on the mild little chestnut her parents had purchased for her.

Davy would have helped, only Pippa kept Davy and the horses away from each other. The boy had no fear, but Pippa had fear for Davy. He had to have a restricted life, and a pony ride was one of those many restrictions.

'At least get on Billy Boy, Marilyn,' pleaded Pippa.

'No.'

'At least pat him.'

'He'll bite me.'

'He won't. He likes apples to bite, not little girls.'

'In fact he's frightened of little girls,' said a voice, and Crag Crag joined the group. 'I have the same trouble sometimes up at Falling Star with the piccaninnies.' Crag looked at Marilyn. 'Do you know piccaninnies?'

'Yes,' Marilyn said.

'Well, my scrubbers . . . do you know scrubbers?'

'No.'

'I can tell her.' It was Davy by Crag's side, but then where else would Davy, given the chance, be?

He proceeded to do so.

'Only these are scrubbers who've learned better.' Crag took on from Davy. 'They've learned enough to go after other scrubbers. See?'

'Yes. But I still wouldn't like them.' Marilyn wrinkled her nose. 'They're dangerous.'

'They think *you* are,' corrected Crag. He went up to Billy Boy. 'Look, mate, she won't hurt you. I know how you feel, but she's quite safe.' He turned to Marilyn. 'Silly, isn't it, Billy Boy being scared of you like this.'

'Is he?' Marilyn's eyes were wide.

'Yes. But perhaps I can help him by letting Davy show him how safe children really are.'

Pippa gave a half-step forward.

'Can I? Can I, Crag?' Davy's voice was eager.

'Reckon I'm not your boss, scrubber, your sister's that.'

'She'll say no.'

'Reckon she mightn't.' Crag turned to Pippa and said in such a low voice that only she could hear it: 'Reckon she could feel, that living for ever means rides on ponies, too. Reckon she could if she'd only give it a try.'

Pippa faltered, 'He'll get excited.'

'But he'll enjoy it. Better to fill up a cup even if it overflows than leave it empty.'

'I – I don't know.'

'You know,' he said, waited a moment, then swung Davy into the saddle. Davy was ecstatic. His ecstasy showed so much that Marilyn became querulous.

'It's my pony,' she cried, 'it's my turn!'

Davy was put down and Marilyn was put up.

'That was beaut, Pippa,' Davy said. No harm seemed done.

A lot of good was done for Marilyn. When Dom came over later, Davy and Crag having left, he was pleased with the result.

'It was Mr. Crag really who won the day,' reported Pippa.

'Oh, he's still around, is he?'

'Did you expect him to be gone?'

'He doesn't like the city. He calls the Southern Highlands the city. He never stops longer than he can help. I wonder why he's extending now.' Dom stood silent a moment, his lips pursed.

He came out of his thoughts to ask Pippa if she would come and look at Velvet with him. On his calculations

Velvet was not ready yet, but Velvet had her own ideas.

'If you've any way with cows, Pippa, tell her to hang off, her vet's out of town.'

'You said that picking times like that was a favourite pastime with Velvet.'

'Yes,' sighed Dom. 'It would be just like her to do it again now.'

When they reached the cow her spasm was over and she was contentedly ruminating.

'That's Velvet for you,' said Dom bitterly. 'I really believed she was beginning. I suspect her of staging these alarms especially to keep us on our toes.'

Pippa was squatting beside Velvet, a pretty, rather small cow, who wore a bell locket and had big plum eyes. She examined her as she had seen neighbours in the village examine their cows.

'She mightn't be pulling our legs,' she told Dom, 'she could be on the way. I'd ring that vet if I were you.'

'I rang,' he said dolefully, 'he's out of town.'

'Any other vets?'

'Several in the Highlands, but they're all away. There's a Sydney conference, and seeing it only means a day away from their practices it's being well attended. Also, Velvet was declared only last week as a month off.'

'Could be, too,' agreed Pippa. 'Anyway, she seems all right now.'

'It was just an act she was putting on,' declared Dom determinedly. 'Wasn't getting enough attention. Look here, my girl' . . . to Velvet . . . 'if you moo me back here again, I'll—'

'Moo-oo!' cried Velvet.

'She's an actress,' repeated Dom, 'she has to project herself. Sorry to have brought you along, Pippa, we'll leave this female to chew it over on her own.'

'Moo-oo!' protested Velvet, but they laughed and

went off.

But not far. Velvet gave a very loud 'Moo-oo', and going back just for a final look and an admonishment, Dom called, 'By jove, she's right, Pippa, she's on the way, well on it.'

Pippa hurried to his side. The little cow had got on to the job in a hurry as soon as they turned away. The feet were protruding from the unborn calf.

'It shouldn't be long,' said Pippa, but Dom groaned.

'It could be an hour, more, she's only small but she has big children. The vet was trying to keep the size down, but Velvet's a cunning girl, she's always so proud of herself I wouldn't put it past her rejecting his size-determining medication when our backs were turned again, spitting it out again. This girl knows more than she should.'

He was on his knees, manipulating, massaging, soothing. He kept it up until his arms protested, then Pippa took over.

They did this in turn for well over an hour. Dom was getting worried.

'If only she'd co-operate,' he despaired.

'I think it's a bigger calf than ever before,' Pippa offered, 'I think as you said that Velvet spat out that medication.'

'Can you keep going while I see if Ferguson is back from Sydney yet? I feel this needs more than we can give.'

Pippa nodded, and Dom ran across to the office. He was gone some time, which she knew was not a hopeful sign. Evidently Ferguson was still away, and he was trying other districts.

As she manipulated, massaged, edged downwards, encouraged and persuaded, Pippa saw a car go up to the house. The doctor, she thought, calling on Uncle Preston.

63

She had a sudden idea.

'No go.' Dom was back again. Pippa only gave him time to say that, then she interrupted his explanation again of the city conference with the breathless ... for it was no easy job massaging and manipulating Velvet ... announcement that Doctor Burt was up at Uplands.

Dom caught on at once.

'Of course,' he said. 'Hang on, Pippa.' He was away in a flash.

Pippa was talking to Velvet now, soothing, 'Good girl' ... 'Not long' ... 'Just another try.'

The feet of the unborn calf still stopped there.

'Darling, *try*,' urged Pippa.

Velvet looked reproachfully at her, then gave a large moo-oo, and it was happening at last. There was no need for the thin, disinfected rope that Dom had ready, the little fellow, cow or bull calf Pippa had no time to discover yet, was on the straw floor of the light, airy calving pen. After all that fuss no trouble at all. Also, Pippa said severely to Velvet, not such a remarkable size. Velvet ignored her. She also ignored her plum-eyed baby, which she should have started to lick. Pippa knew from her country days that when a mother did not lick her calf she had to be encouraged to do so by sprinkling a little salt on the baby. Dom had thought of everything; he had the salt at hand.

Pippa bent over to take it up.

'Moo-oo!' called Velvet.

'Yes, pet, you've been wonderful, but just now it's baby's turn.'

Baby's turn! But which baby? For another set of little feet were protruding.

'Twins!' Pippa exclaimed, delighted.

She knew how unusual it was, and longed for someone to help ... and join ...

64

in the miracle. But immediately there was much to do. Too much for one pair of hands. With one arm Pippa held off the first baby, who had got to its feet already and was actually searching clumsily for the teats, and with the other she went through the first ritual again, that massaging, soothing, encouraging. She hoped help would not be long.

It was longer than she anticipated. Had she known Dom would not return for what seemed hours but, of course, wasn't, Pippa knew she could not have coped. She learned later that Uncle Preston had had a minor relapse and Doctor Burt had needed Dom's aid to take him upstairs. As soon as he was able, Dom had told Glen Burt what was happening, and they had hurried back, but by then. ...

The second calf was born, daintier than the first ... a girl? ... and this time, without salt, Velvet was licking her child. The first one had found the teats and was sucking contentedly.

'You clever Velvet,' Pippa awarded, 'a Silk and a Satin at the one go. Yes, we'll call them that.'

One arm around the new baby ... the old baby was looking after itself ... and one arm proudly fondled the mother. Elation and triumph shone in Pippa's hillside green eyes, not only the wonder of birth but the miracle of two small offerings. *Two*.

She was laughing maternally, at Silk's floppy wet ears, at Satin's astonished expression, at Velvet's assured look as her tongue darted back and forth in her cleaning duties when the two men came into the calving pen.

She looked up in triumph, waiting for their applause, feeling, with Velvet, the need of a pat, a 'Good girl', a 'Well done.'

They did not speak. Had she stood there, she might have been silenced, too, in the moving picture of a soft-eyed girl and a cow and two calves. And life itself.

But instead she sat waiting, wondering uneasily was something wrong? something amiss?

At that moment Rena, who had caught up with the men, pushed past them, took a long hard look at the scene, then said thinly, 'You can come with me to the house, now, Pippa. I need you there.'

CHAPTER FOUR

As Pippa walked from the stables back to Uplands beside her cousin she darted a nervous look at the cold, set face. Nervous, because Rena's tone had insinuated a reckoning, and although Pippa had never found herself in such a position with Rena, all at once she was remembering with distaste Janet's warning, ex-schoolmate Janet who once must have crossed swords with her cousin because she had warned: 'Leopards don't change their spots.'

Rena was not beautiful now, she noted, or if she was it was hard to find beauty in that bleak look. What on earth had she done, Pippa wondered, for Rena to be furious with her like this?

She must have wondered it aloud, though she hadn't intentionally formed the words, for Rena stopped abruptly, stopping Pippa with her, and accused, 'You're the sly one, aren't you? Timed that beautifully, didn't you? Arranged yourself sweetly, made everything look your doing—'

'What are you talking about, Rena?'

'As though you don't know!'

'I don't . . . unless you mean . . .'

'I mean the happy event. Happy, anyway, for you.'

'Oh, Rena, don't exaggerate, I had no idea that Velvet was going to—'

'But Velvet did, didn't she, and you acquitted yourself admirably, didn't you, and – and—' Rena's voice cracked.

'I should think you would be pleased I was there,' endeavoured Pippa. 'After all, calves are an asset to a farm, and—'

Rena gave a dismissive gesture. 'Oh, that,' she put aside. 'Anyone would think you were being merely farm-minded.'

'I was. What else?' – But even as she asked it, Pippa put herself in Rena's place, and she knew how Rena felt.

In Rena's opinion she had 'upstaged' Rena . . . that had been Dom's phrase . . . because Rena herself had wanted to score on the maternal angle, paint a pretty picture with the help of Davy to impress the doctor, but Pippa had beaten her to it and of all things with two calves. The absurdity of the position brought a laugh to her lips.

'Rena, you're quite ridiculous. How appealing could I possibly look squatted down beside a cow? How on earth could Doctor Burt—'

'Doctor Burt?'

Rena looked at her quite stupidly for a long moment, looked at her as though she didn't understand her. Then she said, 'It wasn't that, it was your know-allness with Dom Hardy. He would appreciate that. He would like a girl who was resourceful.'

'Of course he would. He's a land-man and—'

'And you're a land-woman.'

'No more than I was a nurse. I wish you'd make up your mind what I was, more than that what you want me to be, because I'm certainly confused, Rena. I just don't understand.'

'There's nothing to understand,' Rena said dully.

'The way I see it there is,' persisted Pippa. 'Not only must I watch my step with Glen Burt for you, it seems to me I must also keep my distance from Mr. Hardy.'

'I never said so. I – I—'

'But you've just criticized me for helping him.'

'Nothing of the sort. I – why, I loathe the man. You have a vivid imagination, Pippa, but then your father was a poet.'

'It was Davy who took after our father,' said Pippa quietly. She asked: 'Where is Davy? Did Doctor Burt see him?'

'Not yet. He was to, but Father suddenly had this thing.'

'Badly?'

'No. Just a minor turn. He's in bed now, and will stop there a day or so. I think it's just a case of trying to make up for his last rest. Every minute must pay. That's typical of Daddy.' She paused. 'Davy should be around somewhere.'

Pippa asked could she help now with Uncle Preston, but was told no. Considering that ostensibly she had been brought up from the calving pen for this explicit cause, Pippa felt like demanding the real reason why she was here. Really, Rena would be restricting everyone soon. She turned to demand an explanation, but found to her surprise that Rena's lips were thinned no longer, but full and soft and trembling. Her lovely eyes were bright with unshed tears.

'Why, Rena—'.

'Oh, go away. *Go away*!'

Pippa went.

She wandered around aimlessly, feeling an anticlimax after the earlier events of the day. She felt she wanted to talk about it all. Uncle Preston's door was closed, so obviously he was resting. She was sorry, because she knew that at least he would have liked to have heard about Velvet, even if the resultant glitter in his eyes was the vision of cents and dollars and not the miracle of birth.

Where was Davy? She looked in his favourite haunts to no avail, then decided to go down to the planting in case he had decided to visit his 'best friend' once more. Only this morning as she had dressed him Davy had spoken proudly of: 'My best friend, Crag Crag.'

She crossed the fields, then plunged into the cool green, not aware that although there was no panic now, Davy knew his way and would not lose himself, that she was running. Then, out of breath, she did realize it, and she stopped abruptly. Why, she demanded of herself, am I hurrying to Crag like this? Is it because he's the only one available to be run to, or is it— No. No, of course it's not.

She made herself turn back.

A voice halted her, and she whirled round again. Crag Crag was standing beneath a pine and watching her.

'The scrubber's not with me, if that's what you've come about,' he said. 'On the other hand, if it is Yours Truly you're after' . . . he pushed the ridiculous ten-gallon hat he wore, ridiculous, anyway, for cool Tombonda, back over his head . . . 'if it's me, I'm here.' He grinned foolishly.

'I – I was looking for Davy.'

'Then he's at the calving. Oh, yes' . . . taking out his pipe and tobacco . . . 'the news has got around. The scrubber was with me when we heard, so we strolled across. He was so enthralled I left him there. After all, birth is a first importance, isn't it? And not just one young feller but twins! Congratulations, Pippa.'

'You should give those to Velvet.'

'I did, but she – and Hardy – referred me to you. You did a fine job, girl.'

'It was an honour,' she said, rather pink with pleasure, 'to be there at the arrival of Silk and Satin.'

'Suitable names,' he agreed. 'You're an artist as well as a midwife. But you'll need to think of something less fal-utin' when my Daisy calves.'

'...aving a blessed event, too?'

'...g Star, not here. And being Falling Star it will

be on a much leaner scale. We run to muscle, not beauty, up top.'

'And you actually have a cow there?'

'Yes. Daisy, as I said. Original, isn't it?' he laughed. 'But having a cow up there *is* original. Most often you don't. But Daisy's a tough old girl. Her offspring may lack your Silk and Satin beauty, but they'll wear.' He packed the pipe, tapped it to his liking, then lit up. 'Were you coming over to see me as well?' he asked.

'No.'

'I don't think that's entirely true. I think you were. I think you wanted to tell me, to shout it. And why not, Pippa? Birth is—'

'A first importance,' she quoted him.

'Yes, but something more.' He searched for words.

'A thousand candles?' she asked.

He shook his head. 'That's reserved for something else. But I tell you this: it's morning's at seven, all's right with the world, isn't it, and that, I believe, is how you're still feeling, and what you want to share. Right, girl?'

It was unbelievable. He couldn't know. He couldn't possibly understand this elation she had. – But he did.

'Yes, Crag,' she said.

They sat down on the cool piney ground. Although even the tallest trees were still comparatively small to the height they would eventually reach they made a sound like the sea.

'I love it.' Crag sat back and sighed contentedly. 'It's the one thing Falling Star never has – pine song. The only time at Yantumara when the wind can gossip like this is after the floods when the tall grasses have sprung up. But here in the planting the breeze and the trees can always talk away the hours, and when the wind changes direction it's like bells. Why are you looking at me like that?'

'You could be my father talking.' She thought of Davy who had inherited her father's gift, and her eyes began to blur.

The deep leaves seemed to draw a veil around them, the air was softly dim. He put out his big hand and placed it across hers. He left it there and she did not withdraw her own fingers. Presently, warmed, the shadow gone, she began telling him about the day's events. The satisfaction she had known. The thrill.

'If only—' she finished.

'If only?'

'If only Rena wasn't angry,' she said unhappily.

'That figures,' he said.

'But she told me it wasn't because of Doctor Burt and – and any "upstaging", and somehow I don't think it was.'

'No?' he encouraged. 'What, then?'

'Somehow I think she was annoyed because I – well, I helped *Dom*.'

'That figures, too,' he said.

'I don't understand.'

'You don't have to, Pippa. Also you don't need to do anything about it ... *until Rena starts restricting me*.'

She looked at him in surprise. 'You're never restricted by Rena.'

'Not yet.'

'Crag, what do you mean?'

'Leave it at that,' he advised. He got up and pulled her after him. 'Coming up to Ku?'

'I came for Davy and you said he'd stopped at the shed.'

'Does it have to be Davy before you come to the house?'

'Yes.' She was still confused at what he had said, that restriction he anticipated, and her answer was curt.

'Well, you're direct enough,' he shrugged. 'It's enough to set me packing my bags again for Yantumara.'

'Why are you stopping this long?' Dom had wondered that. 'You said you only ever stayed briefly.'

'That's right.' In spite of the shade he had pulled the brim of his ten-gallon over his eyes. He seemed about to say something, then he seemed to change his mind. 'Put it down to the scrubber and what goes with him,' he smiled.

'What *can* go with Davy?' Pippa cried brokenly; the comfort she had known a little while ago when he had put his big hand silently over hers was not there now. She turned blindly away, avoiding him, darting back through the planting before he could stop her. By the time she had reached the fields she was composed again. Never must Davy see tears.

Not that Davy would have seen anything except the two little calves. He was down at the calving pen as Crag had said, and he was enchanted.

He walked back to Uplands with Pippa, his little hand warm in hers. He was full of talk about Crag's Daisy up at Falling Star, and how Daisy must have two calves, too. 'At least,' he added. He skipped in his pleasure.

Dom had informed Pippa when she had collected Davy that the vet was expected from Tombonda, having returned from his conference and having been informed of the double birth. Dom then passed on Doctor Burt's congratulations to Pippa for a good job done.

It would have made for complete satisfaction, Pippa thought, had she not dreaded a second scene with Rena. However, when she and Davy entered the house Rena was sweetness itself. She even found an opportunity to explain her behaviour to Pippa. 'I was worried over Father,' she said, and had Pippa not been so anxious to accept this, she could have thought that it was the first time that Rena had ever shown such concern.

But when later she was permitted to visit Uncle Preston, she was ashamed of any doubts. He looked ill, more ill than she had anticipated by that 'minor turn' of his daughter.

She sat by his bedside and told him all about Velvet, and as she had thought he was very pleased.

'At the price of calves,' he said, 'that makes...' He stopped his calculations to ask: 'Not identical twins, I hope?'

'No, Uncle, a cow and a bull calf. Why do you hope against identicals?'

'They're taken automatically by the Scientific Breeding Group for further study. The fee for unidenticals by private sale is much more to my liking.'

'You and your money!' she teased him.

'It's all too true, Pippa.' He pleated the top of the sheet with thin fingers; he had lost a lot of weight. 'That last investment of mine was a wrong 'un, the first you could say in all my life. What a time to pick to mess things up! But then I've messed things all through. A man doesn't see that when he's doing it, only when it's done, and it all lies there behind him like a book with its pages upturned. I messed up Rena. She's spoiled. She'll never be able to take what's coming now.'

'Uncle Preston, I'm sure you exaggerate.'

'Then that makes you and my girl too. The trouble was I lost my touch, I took my finger off the button, you might say, when I let Rena persuade me to leave the city and settle down here. Things ... *my* things haven't gone well since.'

'This place is thriving.'

He shrugged irritably. 'That's Hardy's kingdom, not mine. Did you know, Pippa, that it was because of Hardy that we initially came to Uplands?'

Pippa had not known. Having only met with these relations so recently she had taken it for granted that Uplands had always been their home. Or one of their homes.

'Oh, yes,' said Uncle Preston, 'it was only after my girl met Dom Hardy in England a few years ago that it became top of her list. I had the idea for a while ... I really thought ... I hoped ...' His voice trailed off and he was silent a moment.

'But Dom Hardy isn't English, Uncle.' Pippa broke into his thoughts.

'He was taking a trip, a "gen" trip he called it. You must have noticed how English-like are these Southern Highlands of New South Wales. Hardy noticed and was taking farming tips.'

'And you met him?'

'*Rena* and I met him.' A pause. 'Straightway that girl had a new theme.'

'A farm.'

'That's it.' Uncle Preston laughed indulgently, but he cut the laugh short. 'There I go again, always spoiling her. I shouldn't laugh over my own mistakes.'

'So you chose one that Dom recommended?' asked Pippa.

Uncle Preston nodded. 'It quite suited me apart from Rena insisting on it. Not so far from Sydney so that I couldn't keep my finger on the button ... or so I thought. But a business man needs to keep the button right there beside him, not three hours away. I found that out. Either I slipped in my judgment or—'

'Does it matter, Uncle Preston?' Pippa asked gently. 'Does a little less money matter?'

'That wasn't all the judgment I lost,' he said bluntly. 'You see, I thought ... I was sure ... But I was wrong.'

Pippa herself thought that never until she had come to

Tombonda had she heard so many conundrums. Dom uttered them. Crag did. Now Uncle Preston was saying them. And they were all to do with Rena. What was it about Rena?

To divert the old man she began telling him about her riding episode earlier in the week, and how she had foolishly taken the horse down to the gully.

He nodded, but she could see he was not attending . . . that is until she finished ruefully with her tumble, and, for conversation, how Rena had advised her afterwards that sometimes it was not just the ground that was hard.

'She said that?' he came in quite sharply, and the sharpness surprised Pippa.

'Yes, Uncle Preston.' She looked wonderingly at him.

'What else did that girl of mine say?'

'That was all. She just said that it was not always the ground that was hard.'

He was quiet for a while, then he mused: 'She fell herself once, you know.'

'Yes, you told me. You said that after that she was—'

'She was more Rena than before,' he finished for Pippa. 'More capricious. More self-willed. Less what I was hoping, hoping for her and—' He closed his eyes for a moment, then opened them again. 'She even got an urge to leave here, leave Uplands. But for once I didn't indulge her. I felt I had moved enough, that I was too old to begin again. Pippa' . . . abruptly . . . 'what do you think of Hardy?'

'Your overseer?'

'Yes. What do you think of him, girl?'

'He's great,' Pippa said warmly, if a little surprised at the sudden turn in the conversation.

'Apart from that would you say he was – well, a stubborn kind of fool?'

76

'Never a fool, Uncle Preston.'

'But stubborn? Proud? Determined?'

'Yes, all of those,' Pippa nodded. 'Very stubborn, proud, determined.'

Another silence crept into the room. It was so long that Pippa suspected the old man had fallen asleep. She sat on for a while, wondering whether to tiptoe out or wait for him to wake up again.

He settled it for her.

'I'm awake, girl, but don't stay on.'

'No, Uncle Preston.' She got up. 'Anything you want?'

Uncle Preston said an odd thing, and Pippa was to remember it afterwards.

He said: 'You've given it to me. Close the door after you. Thanks.'

The next day Pippa met Glen Burt. Already Davy had become friends with him, telling his sister that he was a pretty good vet ... Pippa told herself she must have a word with Crag Crag about that ... and that he intended to do what the doctor told him, because Crag's Manager had done that and look what Crag's Manager had won. — Always Crag came into it, Pippa sighed.

'Yes, darling,' she nodded, 'but please not vet.'

'I told Doctor Glen and he didn't seem to mind.'

No one seemed to be minding, not even Rena when she presented her doctor to Pippa. She was all sweet concern, tender solicitude. Almost Pippa could have convinced herself that that warning that Rena had issued to her regarding the young medico was imagination.

The meeting was in Davy's room, Rena sitting at the window with the little boy, and looking lovely enough, Pippa thought, to stir anyone's heart. But Doctor Burt's attention was only on Davy, a fact that Rena should have

77

appreciated as a point against Pippa even though at the same time it would have to be considered as something against herself. When, after a quick check of the child, the doctor gave Rena a meaning look, Rena rose at once, the perfect intuitive nurse, and took Davy outside. That she stopped in the garden where she could be seen as she lovingly and very winningly tended the little boy dimmed none of her touching devotion.

Glen Burt said, 'I haven't had an opportunity to commend you on your handling of that cow, Miss Bromley. You seemed to know what you were about.'

'I was a country girl.'

'Still, not all country people. . . . You weren't working for an English veterinarian, by any chance?' He smiled, and added, 'I know from your cousin that you're not a nurse.'

Pippa supposed that that would be one of the things that Rena would take care to tell him. 'No, I wasn't,' she said, 'I was a clerk.'

'I was hoping from your coolness that you might have been one of our brigade.'

'Either animal, vegetable, mineral,' she laughed, and he laughed with her, but his good-looking face soon becoming serious again.

'I really meant,' he explained, 'that you might be able to give me some data on Davy.'

'But I can do that, of course.'

His smile was polite now. 'Of course . . . though what I wanted—'

She understood that he did not mean the usual surface details but deeper personal medical points, and who knew Davy better than Davy's sister? In a quiet, concise manner she tabulated everything she had learned from Doctor Harries about Davy. Doctor Burt listened intently, nodding his dark head now and then.

'Thank you,' he said when she had finished. 'That's what I wanted but scarcely expected.'

'Davy is all I have,' she said, 'so I had to know.'

There was a silence as Glen Burt made notes in a small book.

Pippa steeled herself to say, 'I know already that for Davy it's prognosis nil, Doctor.'

He looked up from the book and answered, 'I wish I could deny that.'

'But you can't.'

'Instead of saying No I'll say that sometimes in spite of facts, in spite of all a doctor knows, it doesn't always happen as a doctor believes.'

'Thank you.' Her smile was bleak. With an effort she said conversationally, 'Rena has told me that your ambition is research.'

He closed the book, then nodded to Pippa. 'Being a G.P., particularly a country one, will be something that will always be immensely valuable to me, but I have to admit that research is the only thing I really want.'

'Then you'll be leaving the district at some time?'

He smiled faintly. 'It takes money for that kind of dream.'

Pippa remembered Rena's: 'Glen wants to do research. That costs money, and you'd think he'd be aware that I could help him.' Instinctively her glance flicked outward to the golden girl on the lawn, now kneeling beside Davy to adjust the strap of his sandal.

The doctor saw the glance. Quietly, so quietly she could almost have imagined it, he said, 'No.'

'What, Doctor Burt?'

'Thank you for your concise information on your brother. I receive new reading every day, and I shall be on the alert especially now for anything pertaining to Davy.'

79

'Yes,' she said, but knowing, as he knew, that he had not answered her question.

They joined the others on the lawn.

When the doctor had gone, Rena changed her role of nurse to Davy to that of examiner of Pippa. She demanded what, where, how.

'It was all medical talk, Rena.'

'I expected it to be.' Rena's mouth thinned. She added, 'But tell me all the same.'

'He just said that Davy . . .' Pippa had to turn away.

Rena at least had the grace not to press her, but she still waited, so Pippa repeated Glen Burt's remark on wanting research but not having the money.

'You see,' triumphed Rena.

Pippa did not proceed to that odd 'No' from the doctor when his glance had followed her glance, she let Rena bask in the assurance of her money and what it could do. But most of all her cousin seemed to find delight in the fact that research would take Glen . . . and his wife as a matter of course . . . right away.

'*Right away*,' Rena repeated, almost hugging the words.

'But, Rena, you go away often. You could go now.'

'But I'd be expected back. This is my home. This is where I live with my father. When you're married, you belong to the one you're married to, so you don't come back, you're not expected. It would have been no good with Crag, for he returns regularly to Ku, and always will. I have to be away. *Away*.'

'But why?' Pippa looked at her, confused. 'You can't dislike the place, for you chose it.'

Rena had gone quite white. 'Yes, I chose it, but now I hate it. I hate it!' Almost choking on that last 'hate', Rena turned and left.

Glen Burt attended Uncle Preston several times during

the following week, and on each occasion had a look at Davy. He had an idea to try him on remedial exercises, but was very anxious to select the right ones, for he believed that wrong movements could deter the boy.

Rena offered sweetly to supervise these exercises, and who more able, Pippa thought; she had had the most expensive ballet tuition.

'No, Davy's sister, I think. The way she reported Davy to me I knew she understood even Davy's smallest muscle. This is what I'm after, Miss Bromley.' He had drawn a stick figure to demonstrate, and beckoned Pippa over. With a sinking heart, for she had glimpsed the quick look in Rena's face, Pippa tried to follow the text.

As far as she could see it ran the same gamut as the things that Crag often recommended. Crag wanted Davy to step out of himself, be more the boy and less the small ornament, or so he expressed it, only there to be touched gently, dusted and replaced. He had said, Pippa recalled, that little scrubbers had nothing in the past to regret and nothing in the future to fear, meaning, she interpreted, that Davy should live more *ordinarily*, and that was what Glen Burt, in medical terms, was saying now.

Part of the exercises involved walking while practising deep breathing. Pippa selected this one and took Davy across to Ku. – Or at least they started in that direction. As they passed through the planting she assured herself that it was because Davy was so eager for this particular exercise and so lacklustre as regarded the arm flinging and toe touching, which, after all, was only childlike, that she had chosen it, but when Davy acclaimed delightedly, 'You're skippety-hoppity, too,' of her twinkling progress, she could not deny it.

'It's the pine needles,' she told him.

'No, it's Crag,' he said. 'You're wanting to see him like I am. I love the pine needles, though, and I'll miss them up at Falling Star.'

About to argue that it was not Crag, Pippa said urgently instead: 'Darling, we're not going to Falling Star.'

Her brother answered, unconsciously adopting Crag's slow, deliberate drawl, 'I reckon we might, though, because that's what my best friend is waiting back for.'

Pippa halted, and halted Davy with her.

'I think we'll see the calves instead,' she said abruptly.

Davy was in a predicament. Silk and Satin of the wet noses and insecure legs or his best friend? His best friend would still be his best friend, he must have decided, but Silk and Satin grew every time you looked at them, and soon, according to Dom, they would be almost as big as their mother, the bull calf even bigger. Davy said judiciously, 'I think Crag will understand,' and agreed to be led instead another way, also to co-operate with deep breathing.

While he fondled the twins, the mother looking on implacably, Dom showed Pippa the gymkhana programme for the forthcoming Southern Highlands Pony Gathering.

'I'll be entering in practically every event,' he said, 'and I'm counting on you to stable for me.'

'I'm glad you didn't say ride. I didn't do so well last time, did I?'

'This wouldn't be down a valley,' he smiled, 'but in the parklands of the Pony Club, which are as smooth as a billiard table. Also, the owners of the ponies will be doing most of the riding themselves. Nevertheless there will be some events, Pippa, that perhaps—'

She smiled back and half-agreed, then joined Davy in the adoring of the small animals.

On Doctor Burt's insistence a nurse had been brought

in for Uncle Preston. Pippa had heard Rena protesting to Glen that she could manage her father herself, but he had stood firm, suggesting gently but adamantly that she was too close to Preston Franklin to be of real impersonal value, and in nursing an impersonal approach was a very essential thing.

Rena had been unsure whether to pout or take the doctor's ruling as a compliment to her as a devoted daughter, and while she had hesitated, Glen Burt had contacted a nursing bureau and succeeded in engaging Sister Bruce, a reliant person with sufficient years to assure Rena that her hesitancy had been a right move.

Rena now concentrated on Davy, and was always with him whenever the doctor called.

It was simply too much, Pippa thought. Surely Rena, an intelligent girl, must see that she was overdoing it, must sense eventually that she could never win with such obvious tactics. Undoubtedly if you loved a man you had every right in the world to fight for him, but when was possessing a fair fight? Then did Rena really love Glen? *Did* Rena?

Pippa could not have said why she held that doubt, Rena had said a hundred times how she felt to Glen, but still the feeling persisted, that feeling that Rena was forcing, or trying to force, the issue, forcing it with more urgency than emotion, and because of this when the young doctor spoke to Pippa as he did, Pippa did not feel so distressed as she might have had she felt that her cousin really cared.

Glen drew Pippa into the garden following one of his visits ... Rena on the mats she especially had sent for and doing gradual push-ups with Davy, and looking, and no doubt aware of it, very lovely as she did so ... and began with a tentative: 'What do you think of this exercise régime?'

'I suppose anything that builds up strength must be of some benefit,' Pippa said.

'Yes.'

There was a pause, then:

'Miss Bromley . . . Pippa . . .'

'Yes, Doctor Burt?'

'Could you say Glen?'

'Yes, Glen.'

'I . . . Well . . .' Another pause.

'Yes, Glen?'

'It's difficult to put into words.'

'Davy?' she said hollowly. How often had she said her brother's name tonelessly like that?

'Oh, no.' He hastened to reassure her. 'It's – Rena. Much as I dislike any such move I – I feel I must give up your uncle and your brother as my patients.'

'But, Doctor – but, Glen—'

He poked at a blade of grass with the toe of his shoe. He seemed wretched, but nonetheless determined to say what had to be said.

'Why does she go on like that?'

About to pretend that she didn't understand him, instead Pippa said quietly: 'Rena?' She knew he was aware that she understood his trend.

'Yes, Pippa. She . . . oh, this is very embarrassing for me.'

'Can love be embarrassing, Glen?'

'Rena doesn't love me, any more than I love her, but for some reason she – well, she—'

'Yes,' nodded Pippa. Again she spoke quietly.

'But, Glen,' she said presently, 'you're a doctor, your work comes first. Oh, I can understand how you feel, but – well—' She searched for words, found none, so made a little helpless gesture towards her brother.

'I can't work as I want to work with Miss Franklin

acting as she does,' he said bluntly. 'I'm a dedicated person, Pippa, I always have been. I have no time for all this.' He spread thin sensitive hands.

'Rena could find you time.' Pippa felt she was entitled to say that, for hadn't Rena already said it? 'She has enough to let you follow the path you want to, Glen.'

'But I wouldn't want it. Not without . . .' He turned to Pippa. 'You see, there's someone else. She was at university with me. Nothing has ever been said between us, otherwise I would have said it to your cousin, but the way I feel about Jennifer and the way I sense she could feel about me . . .'

There was a pause, then Glen Burt spoke again.

'We never actually discussed things, but we both knew what we wanted from our years of study, and I believe we both knew whom we wanted it with. It's Jennifer some day, I hope, Pippa. It *has* to be Jennifer. – So you see how I feel now.'

'You said before that Rena was only playing a part with you, then wouldn't that make it easier for you to tell her what you have just told me?'

He gave another movement of his hands. 'Is anything easy with Rena?' he asked. Then he said the same as Crag had said. 'How can you tell her when she's running away?'

'Running away, Glen?'

'I feel that. I suppose I'm crazy.'

'Someone else said it. But – but from whom?'

Almost as if answering the question Domrey Hardy joined the two of them on the lawn.

They talked a while, then, believing that Dom wished to consult Rena on farm matters, Pippa nodded to the two exercisers, but Dom did not even glance in that direction.

'It was you I wanted to see, Pippa, that is if the doctor

is finished . . .'

'I'm finished.' There was the slightest sigh in Glen's voice as he turned back to Rena and Davy again. What an odd position, Pippa thought, here was a lovely and a richly-endowed girl, yet neither of these two men— Rather grateful herself to get out of the tangle, even if only temporarily, Pippa walked beside Dom back to his office.

'What is it, Dom? More blessed events?' There were still unfulfilled dates on the calendar.

'No, Pippa, nothing immediately imminent. I just want to speak with you about the forthcoming show.'

'The Pony Gathering.'

'Actually it's more than that, it's a bit of everything, though I must admit the horses dominate it. There's the usual events, the usual judging, also a dog section, a cat division, and those delightful displays of jams and cakes competing for blue ribbons.'

'Is that what you wanted to tell me about, Dom?' she laughed.

'No, but you're entitled to enter,' he assured her. 'How are you on scones with wings?'

'They invariably crash,' she told him ruefully, 'my aunt did the cooking.'

'Well, perhaps the handiwork,' he smiled. 'Seriously, though, I'll be calling upon you to help out in some of the events.'

She nodded that she would, adding, 'But nothing fancy.'

'I did hope to put Suzy in the Steeple. Oh, it's a very restricted steeple,' he hastened to reassure her.

'Still too wild for me.'

'That's a pity. Suzy's a born hunter.'

They had reached the office by now, and he drew up a chair and handed Pippa a programme of events. They were very comprehensive. She noted, too, that the gathering was everything Dom had said. It went from flowers and produce, preserves and children's handwriting right through the usual gamut to finish up (after pigs, dogs, cats and cattle had been dealt with) at the real reason for the gathering: horses. There would be, Pippa read, the expected stalls and sideshows, coconut shies and wood chops. Even a merry-go-round was offering, Dom smiled, for the less heroic equestrian. He looked obliquely at Pippa as he said this, and, seeing his trend, she protested again that she would help him out in every other way but that she still didn't feel skilled enough for a steeple.

'Minor steeple.'

'It's still a jump. What about this event? And this? I'll even try this one.'

The morning of the gathering dawned blue and gold. It gave an early promise to grow into one of those flawless, brilliant days that the mild Southern Highlands so often puts on. Already there was a breeze with a pleasantly exciting edge to it that would flutter all the ribbons and flags. It would also tatter the tossed lolly wrappers and peanut shells, Uncle Preston said typically as Pippa said good-bye to him, but he had a smile about him for all his acid words . . . a satisfied smile that Pippa was to remember later.

Childlike, Davy was almost hugging himself with delight. Feeling the old magic of all-fairs-wherever-they-be-herself, Pippa held the little hand in hers and squeezed it as they passed through the turnstile.

The pony events were not programmed until after lunch, so Pippa and Davy did the rounds of the mouth-watering cake marquee, the mysterious fortune-teller, the fascinating fat lady, the frustrating Aunt Sally. Pippa was just heading for the handicraft, having bribed Davy who was not so keen on this with a cornet of spun sugar, when her small brother glimpsed something . . . or somebody as Pippa soon discovered . . . and darted away.

As she might have known the attraction was Crag Crag, even more wonderful to a wide-eyed small boy today in his black singlet, white pants, white boots and *standing by an axe*.

'Davy, come back!' she called urgently.

Crag, waiting beside a block of wood as were five others in the small arena, smiled at her and assured her, 'It's all right, the scrubber won't come to any harm. I'll send him off at Seconds Out, for I reckon he's my second. Are you, scrubber?'

'Oh, yes, Crag. What do I do, Crag?'

'You can pick up those few chips around my block, see to it that my sweat rag is ready.'

'Davy—' feared Pippa.

'He's all right,' Crag assured her again.

'But when you start chopping . . . you are going to, aren't you?'

'Reckon that's what I'm here for. Don't worry, Pippa, there's no danger, the stewards will put round a cordon, and anyway, woodmen place their chops.'

'But you're not a woodman.'

'No,' he agreed, 'but I do a bit up top, and it's on harder stuff than this.' He looked down at his log.

Pippa restrained herself from crying out 'Davy' again when her brother busily dusted the axe. The little boy was blissful, he fussed around Crag like a mother hen, but for all his excitement when the stewards called 'Seconds Out', he went at once at a nod from Crag to Pippa's side.

The adjudicator warned, 'Three seconds, gentlemen. One. Two . . .' Then the chop began.

Crag was slow off the mark and when he did start he

seemed to have a stolid pace. There was none of the quicksilver of the other competitors, the effortless rhythm, he just lumbered along.

'Crag,' Davy was calling, 'Crag!' And all at once Pippa heard herself calling it, too.

Then something happened. The lumbering pace changed to a swinging cut. Instead of standing upright, Crag now almost crouched over the log. By the time he reversed he had passed two of the other five and his chips were flying fast.

'Crag!' called Davy.

'Crag,' called Pippa. 'Crag . . . Crag!'

For a breath of a second, so infinitesimal it must have been imagination, the man looked up and across at Pippa, then at once the great chunks of wood were rising, the racing axe was flailing through the air as though wielded by a machine and not a man.

Then he was through.

Even had he not jumped apart to prove it, everyone would have known by Davy's shouts of joy that he had won. – Pippa's, too, only she was not aware of them.

But she was aware of Crag coming across with a trophy and putting it in Davy's hands, of his saying, 'Thanks, scrubber, I reckon the way you shouted for me it was you who won it.'

But looking at Davy's sister.

They had lunch together in the tea pavilion, Davy refusing to be parted from the large silver cup and having difficulty in managing his lemonade and sandwiches with its gleaming bulk enclosed in one protective arm.

After the break the gymkhana began. Pippa left Davy with Crag and took up her duties for Dom Hardy. A sheepdog trial, a tent-pegging, a camp draft were staged, then the races began.

Pippa won a red ribbon and two yellow ones for Dom's

stable in age classes, but once again refused the steeple. He smiled and took it philosophically, but she felt he was disappointed.

She went out to see if Davy was still with Crag, and after much searching found the pair of them leaning over the course railing and shouting encouragement to Rena. Rena was with the other steeple entrants at the starting post. *On Suzy.*

'What's Rena doing—' Pippa began, but the pistol stopped her query. The chase had begun.

Right from the beginning Rena left the others well behind. She rode faultlessly. She also rode contemptuously, and Pippa glanced up at Dom who now had joined them by the fence, and saw his tightened lips.

Her cousin won with ease. She was off the mount and handing him carelessly to Dom, when Pippa, remembering her strapper duties, came hurrying across.

'No falling off this time,' she heard Rena say in a hard bitter voice, 'no mistakes and no reckless words to be corrected by Mr. Hardy.'

'Rena—' Pippa heard Dom say tensely back. 'Rena—'

What would have happened then? Pippa was to wonder this afterwards. Would Dom have gone on from that tense 'Rena—' . . . would he have—

But she was not to know, for through the loudspeaker someone else called for Rena, called: 'Wanted at the office urgently, Miss Franklin. Miss Franklin, please.'

It was Crag who came up to Pippa to say quietly: 'Go with her.'

'But—'

'Go, Pippa,' Crag repeated. He assured her: 'I've got the scrubber.'

By the time Pippa reached the office, Rena had been told.

Told that a message had come from Uplands. Her father had died.

CHAPTER FIVE

THERE could be no doubt about Rena's grief. Pippa, who often had felt herself instinctively withdrawing from her cousin because of her apparent callous lack of relationship with her father, now saw that it all had been a façade, that the bond had been so tight that it had needed no word, no gesture, no daughterly embellishment.

Hours after the gymkhana announcement, and after the exhausting floods of tears had been released, Rena had sat up in the bed in which Pippa had placed her and said woodenly, 'We were one, Pippa; now he's gone I'm not whole any more, it's an amputation.'

Pippa, murmuring the usual consolations, was stopped imperatively by Rena's impatient hand on her arm.

'*One*,' she repeated. 'I'm as selfish as he was. We both thought only of ourselves.'

'You're wrong, Rena, Uncle Preston thought all the time of you.'

'Then he was thinking of himself, for we were the same. And now . . .' Again the tears flowed.

Pippa felt those tears could do more for her cousin than she could, and went out quietly. She was relieved that Crag had taken Davy to stop at Ku. Uplands was no place just now for the child, not with Rena's grief so evident. – Not with the close association of death.

Death. She stood in the garden and thought about it . . . and Davy. She was sad for Uncle Preston. For all his brusque ways, the occasionally awful things he had said, she had liked him. But Uncle Preston had not been a little boy who had only known a handful of springs. Tears stung at her, and she was crying softly and brokenly when Dom Hardy found her.

He put his arm around her and guided her to the barn; he seemed to know instinctively the needed thing to do. In the barn they spent some time on Silk and Satin, and Dom told her how he expected the other blessed events at any moment. It was good therapy, and she soon was talking back with him. Then suddenly, without any warning, he broke into their exchange with a terse: 'How is she?'

'Rena?'

'Yes.'

'Taking it hard.'

'I expected that.'

'I didn't.' Pippa had found by this time that she could be frank with Dom. 'I thought—'

'That's Rena,' he nodded. 'But it's all a veneer, Pippa, and under that skin . . .' He stopped abruptly to catch a quick breath. From the look in his face there was pain in him.

'Dom . . .' Pippa began, but Dom was on the stock again, talking briskly, and she knew she could not break in.

Doctor Burt had not been out to Uplands since his last attention on Preston Franklin, but sedatives had arrived for Rena, and the nurse had stayed on for a further period.

A message had come for Pippa from Crag that he was keeping Davy with him, and she was grateful about that, for the funeral had been set for the following day.

After it was over and the girls back in the house again, Pippa carried tea to the sun-room and sat with her cousin. She had previously steeled herself to say: 'What now, Rena?' for after all she had to know her future. She had Davy to think of.

'Daddy,' Rena shrugged, 'always said there was no

money.' She gave a little disbelieving laugh. 'That would be typical of Preston Franklin, my parent was always cautious. However, I don't believe it. There may have been a moderate recession, but there would still be a fair amount. Also there's this house.' She glanced around her.

'Yes, I don't think you need worry about finance, Rena.' Pippa meant that. For all his statements to the contrary, she had never taken seriously Uncle Preston's plaints of impending disaster, only his standards of disaster.

'It will make me free,' said Rena, much in the same manner as she had spoken once before, 'free to leave here, leave the Highlands.' She took out her cigarettes and lit up.

When she spoke next she seemed to be addressing the blue weave of smoke . . . anyway, she did not meet Pippa's glance.

'I won't be dependent on anyone else to get me away. Not Crag. Not Glen. – By the way' . . . a brief laugh . . . 'that last fell through. I think you know, Pippa.'

'Doctor Burt?'

'Yes. In a very discreet way our young doctor began referring to this former love of his.'

'Jennifer.'

'Yes. Quite a touching little story. Young students together. No words ever spoken but the feeling there.' Now Rena was back to form, her sharp astringent form.

Uncomfortably, Pippa inserted, 'I don't think you were really hurt, Rena.'

Rena narrowed her eyes on her cousin and said, 'And why should you think that?'

'No reason, except—'

'Except?' Rena demanded.

'Except I don't believe you ever loved him.'

93

'Very intuitive, aren't you? Well' . . . a deliberate yawn . . . 'you were right. He was attractive, of course, but Glen to me was primarily escape, escape from here. Oh, I know you think I could have gone whenever I liked, and I did go for periods, but because of Daddy I had to come back. And Preston Franklin' . . . she had the habit of calling her father by his full name . . . 'for all his regrets at having left Sydney, was still for some reason very much against returning again, from leaving here.'

'Probably his state of health, his age,' suggested Pippa.

'Perhaps.' A shrug. 'All I know is he wouldn't go. So I was tied down, too. But now . . .' She exhaled, and once more gave that little scornful laugh.

'Where will you go, Rena?' – Where will *we* go, was more what Pippa wanted to cry out, where can I take Davy?

'Here . . . there . . . who knows? Oh, you're worrying about the boy, aren't you? Don't fret, I won't see you stuck. As a matter of fact I wouldn't be surprised if Daddy hasn't seen to that in the will. Did I tell you it's to be read almost at once? In the morning, in fact.'

'No, Rena, you didn't.'

'It appears Mr. Callow, our solicitor, is anxious to start the proceedings at once. Rather surprising. Usually the wheels of the law grind painfully slow, or so I've been told. Though probably he's guessed my burning anxiety.' Another little laugh. 'Anxiety to leave.'

Rena got up and went to the window, looked out on the rolling, green, almost parklike qualities of the Highlands terrain, at the ordered perfection of it, then cried, 'Oh, to leave here! To leave here. How I hate the place!'

Yet when she turned back a moment later her eyes were dull and her lips set.

Rena seeming to have control of her grief now, as soon as lunch was over Pippa walked through the planting to Ku to visit Davy.

But when she got there, there was no sign of her brother.

'Mustering,' grinned Crag Crag, who opened the door to her, 'if you can call our small handful a mob. But the scrubber rushed the opportunity to bring the five of them back from the west paddock. He reckoned it would be good practice for later on.'

'Should he?' worried Pippa, making the mustering her first concern. 'Should you have let him?'

'He wanted to,' said the brown man, 'WANTED. I reckoned it would have done him more harm not allowing that want.'

'Perhaps.' Pippa thought of the guarded existence Davy had had in England and how it had done nothing for him. If Crag wished to work on the principle that since it had done no good this could do no worse, then she supposed she could let him. With a sigh she dismissed that concern to take out a second one.

'You shouldn't let him think like you do,' she remonstrated.

'About practising mustering for later on?'

Later on. She found she could not answer that for the rising lump in her throat, for the hopeless knowledge that Davy would never muster anywhere, but she did manage to murmur, 'About visiting you at Falling Star, because a visit is what you sounded like, and of course, we won't be going.'

He was packing his pipe, taking his usual time over it.

'I'd like to talk to you about it,' he said when he had done.

'If it's minding Davy for me up there until things are

finished here, thank you for the offer, and thank you at the same time for all you've done already in minding him, but no.'

'It wasn't that,' he said rather indistinctly, the pipe in a corner of his mouth.

She did not ask him what it was then, for there would be no need to mind Davy; anyway, quite soon, the legal matters would be wound up and she would take over again herself. She told Crag what Rena had said about the will reading. She proffered Rena's guess that there might be a little windfall for Uncle Preston's niece. 'That certainly would be wonderful,' she admitted, 'at least it would get us back to England.'

'And the scrubber miss his second spring?'

'Well, we can't stay here,' she pointed out. 'Rena intends getting rid of the house ... or rather I gathered that.'

'*Whose* house?' A smoke weave must have spiralled up at him, for he had narrowed his eyes on her.

'Hers, of course,' Pippa said irritably, 'Rena's.'

'I see.' Still the narrowed eyes. 'And this will reading, when is it?'

'Tomorrow.'

'I'd go if I were you, Pippa.'

'Oh, no,' she said sensitively. 'It would seem – seem – well, as though I was grasping at anything that Uncle might have left me.'

He smiled a little crookedly at her. 'Left to you, eh? No, that's not what I meant, girl. You just go – for Rena.'

'For Rena?' she asked, puzzled.

'For Rena,' he nodded.

'But—'

'And Pippa—' He paused.

'Yes?'

96

'Come back here after it's over and let me show you a way out.'

'A way out? Really, you do say the oddest things. — How long will Davy be?'

'It depends on how the muster goes.' He lost his serious air and grinned again. He stood up, impelled her upward with him. 'Come and we'll see how our young stockman is doing.'

Davy had completed the chore and was sitting, cowboy-wise, on the fence circling the corral, and regarding his 'muster' the while he chewed on a stem of bittersweet, held much in the manner that Crag held his pipe. Crag . . . Crag . . . what a hero he had made of that man! Uneasily Pippa thought of the wrench it would be when the two friends had to part, yet part they must. Uncle Preston was dead and Rena would be leaving Uplands, her cousins leaving as well. Besides this Crag had spoken many times on how he had outstayed himself here at Ku and how Falling Star needed him. Yes, it could not be long now.

Davy's smile at seeing his sister was quickly wiped off as a thought occurred to him. He said fearfully, 'You didn't come to take me back, did you, Pippa?'

'Not yet, darling, but soon, of course.'

Davy only listened to the first part. He said importantly to the brown man, 'I had a little trouble at the gate, but otherwise all went well. I reckon I'll be of real help to you up at—'

'Davy!' Pippa inserted sharply, but just as sharply Crag came in:

'You didn't drive home that bottom bolt quite enough, scrubber, you always want to make sure of these things,' then, as Davy hurried across to the gate to fix it, he said in a low tone to Pippa: 'No.'

She knew he was remonstrating with her for cutting

into Davy's dreams and she retorted bitterly, 'He mustn't build up like this.'

'Giving in that you could be right about that, though I still won't go along with it, at least wait for a while, girl.'

'Wait? For what?'

He was attending to his eternal pipe. 'Wait for the will,' he said.

'It won't make any difference. Even if Uncle Preston has ... if what Rena said is true ... if there *is* something, I won't be spending it on taking Davy up to—'

'All the same, *wait,*' he said. 'And Pippa, go with her to the reading. She'll need you, I think.'

'How do you come to think these things?' she asked curiously and a little tauntingly. 'Do you have some special knowledge?'

'Only of what *I* would have done had I been Preston Franklin,' he replied cryptically.

She looked at him a long moment, not understanding. But she did not feel like pursuing the subject so instead she called good-bye to Davy. Only that he looked so ecstatically happy, and Davy's happiness must always come first, she might have resented her brother's casual wave in return.

As she walked back through the planting to Uplands she wondered why Crag had asked her to be with Rena tomorrow. She could not go, of course, unless Rena asked her, then if she did ask, *should* she? After all, it was strictly Rena's affair.

But when Rena suggested it that night, she heard herself agreeing to accompany her cousin, and she was angry because it seemed that, like Davy, she was being directed by Crag Crag, and one in the family was enough.

But when Mr. Callow untied the Last Will and Testament of Preston Franklin next morning and read quietly and unemotionally in a dry solicitor voice, she was glad she was with Rena if only to sit there silently beside her. – How, she wondered, had Crag Crag known?

For Rena inherited nothing, yet not because the Franklin estate had dwindled down to that extent *but because she was excluded.*

Mr. Callow put down the papers at last.

'Of course,' he said, 'we will dispute this will.'

'There would not be the slightest doubt,' Mr. Callow went on precisely, 'that your late father's last testament would be proclaimed null and void. The time factor alone between its alteration and his passing would assure that. But even failing this, though I repeat that I have no doubt as to the outcome of an appeal, the appropriate authorities would insist on a re-distribution, and you, as his sole surviving—'

'No!' Rena came in sharply and emphatically. 'No.' She had sat silent until then.

'You are thinking,' interpreted Mr. Callow sympathetically, 'that we would be contesting it on the grounds of your father's mental state at the time of his altering it. You do not want that. I assure you, Miss Franklin, that such a step was not in my mind. It certainly offers a sure way out, but I would have to admit that on the day Mr. Franklin called me to Uplands to attend to this' ... he tapped the sheaf of papers ... 'that he was more alert than I have ever known him. I did attempt to reason with him. After all, what he wanted was quite preposterous. But never have I seen Preston Franklin so adamant, so certain of himself. His income had been receding for some years. Undoubtedly he spoke to you about that?'

'Yes.'

'But there would still have been a comfortable sum for

you, and with the house—'

'Yes. The house.' Rena looked directly at the solicitor. 'To whom was it – sold?'

He hesitated. 'Not sold, Miss Franklin.'

'Then – then given?' But before the solicitor could tell her, Rena said, 'Hardy?'

'Yes.'

'And the rest of Father's goods and chattels and money? To Hardy, too?'

'Yes.'

'Does he know yet?'

'No. I thought it better to tell you first, get you over the initial shock. Of course there won't be any trouble. I know . . . we all know Domrey. All this is going to upset him much more than it upsets you. He'll be more than anxious to have things fixed up as they should be and as soon as possible. As a matter of fact I've been thinking over that mental state again, Miss Franklin. Although to my mind your father had never been more mentally stable, doesn't that prove instability when an only and beloved child is deprived? What I mean to say is—'

'No!' Rena protested again. But this time she even banged the table with her slender white hand to drive home her refusal.

'How much is there?' she asked after a rather startled pause. 'I mean how much – for me?'

Mr. Callow glanced down to his desk. He looked unhappy. 'As I said, the income had plummeted for quite some time.'

'How much?'

'Then without the house,' continued the solicitor, 'and without the grounds—'

'I'm asking you how much?'

A pause. Then: 'Actually only anything in your own name.'

'That's all?'

'Yes.'

'I see.' Rena sat very still. Her face was expressionless.

'Of course,' Mr. Callow hastened to repeat himself, 'it's all too ridiculous to take seriously.'

'My father's last will and testament, Mr. Callow!' Rena rose, and after a moment's hesitation, Pippa rose, too.

Mr. Callow got up.

'You will get in touch with me, Miss Franklin,' he appealed. 'You will go home now and recover from this initial shock.'

'Whose home?' Rena answered, and Pippa remembered Crag asking her the same thing.

'My dear girl, there will be a way out, a way suitable for all concerned. Domrey Hardy—'

'Are you coming, Pippa?' Already Rena was at the door and pushing it open. With a nod to the solicitor she ran down the building steps to her car. 'At least,' she said, opening it up, 'this is mine, it's in my name. The other one, Father's, will be – *his*.'

'Rena—'

'Please, Pippa, not now.'

But Pippa could not contain herself. 'It's so unlike Uncle Preston,' she disbelieved.

'How little you knew him. It's Father exactly. In the same position I probably would have done the same myself.'

'What position?'

But Rena would not answer that.

'Don't you see what he was trying to do?' she said presently. 'Cunning old fox. Cunning old man. Only that old man won't win after all. How far can I get away from here, from Tombonda, on the sale of this car, would you say?'

'Not far,' judged Pippa reluctantly. 'It's not new, and these days—'

But Rena was not listening to her. She was repeating to herself '. . . he knew . . . Father knew . . . but he won't win . . . I—'

'Rena,' cut in Pippa a little desperately, for all at once she was thinking of Davy, 'what can you do?'

Rena took her eyes off the road a moment to look fully at her cousin. 'You really mean what can you do, don't you? I'm sorry, Pippa, sorry to have built you up like that, sorry to have mentioned a bequest, but I really did think . . . ' She laughed wryly. 'How wrong I was!'

'It doesn't matter about the bequest. I only want to know where I stand.'

'Nowhere, like I do. I'm sorry, Pippa' . . . she said again . . . 'but I won't be able to help you at all. You can see how I'm placed myself. I advise you to get the boy, go to Sydney and find a job. There's a surplus of employment there, and you're quite a smart girl.'

'I see,' said Pippa hollowly. Then she asked: 'And you?'

'Don't you worry about me.' Rena's eyes were narrowed. 'I think I may have a solution. And it doesn't include any will-disputing moves, either, or any interviews with the inheritor.' She laughed shortly.

When she drew the car up at the door she just left it there, and ran, without another word for her cousin, into the house.

Pippa did not follow her. What could she say to Rena? Besides, she shivered, she had worries now of her own.

Instinctively she found herself walking across to Ku. Go to Sydney. Find a job. Rena had advised that, and it seemed the only course. But what if Davy were really ill . . . *when* he was really ill . . .

She had not realized she had arrived at the planting

until a hand reached out from one of the pines.

Crag looked down.

He did not take the hand away even after she had let him lead her to a tumbled log, instead he left it there to help her steady herself, and yet, she knew with surprise, I have never felt steadier in my life, even though I don't know what I'm going to do with that life, with Davy's little life, how I'm going to get through all this, still, holding on to Crag, I feel steady.

After several moments he took his hand away and reached for his pipe. He packed and lit it. Then he said: 'You know?'

'The will?'

'Yes.'

'Then I know. But' ... curiously ... 'how did you?'

'I told you, Pippa, it was what I would have done.'

'But why? *Why?*'

He looked at her in wonder. 'You haven't worked that out yet? No' ... a shake of his head ... 'you haven't. Well, it doesn't matter just now. What matters is *us*.'

'Us?' she asked, bewildered.

'You. The Scrubber.' A pause. 'Me.'

'I don't understand.'

'I told you I had a way out, remember, and I reckon you're needing it.'

'I could,' she replied desperately, 'write to Aunt Helen to get us back to England again.' She was remembering the small house, the week-to-week existence, she was knowing how distressed Aunt Helen would be to write back that raising the fares would be beyond her means.

He must have heard her doubt, for he did not even consider the thought.

He said bluntly, without any preamble: 'This is the way out, girl. I said it before on the train coming down to Tombonda, but you thought I was joking ... or showing a damn nerve.

'Well, I was showing a nerve, perhaps, but never joking. I knew what I was asking and I know now.

'Will you marry me, Pippa?'

There was very little wind today, barely enough to stir the pine tops into a sibilant whisper. No ocean in the planting this time, thought Pippa abstractedly, no sound of the sea. The deep leaves had drawn a veil around them. Within that veil she sat and looked at Crag, but understanding what she had just heard. She said so.

'Marriage,' he told her almost gruffly, 'the ceremony or contract by which a man and woman become husband and wife.'

'Yes . . . but why?'

'I could give the usual reason, I suppose,' he said offhandedly. 'Love, isn't it?'

'Yes, but you don't . . . I don't . . .'

'No.' He came in before she could finish it. 'We don't, do we?' He looked at her so long she had to turn her glance away.

'No, we don't,' he confirmed at last. 'But I've heard, and I've read, of other reasons, and they've worked out in the end.'

'Worked out?' she said dully, for it was dull, she thought.

'One of my reasons is the scrubber,' Crag offered. 'In fact he's the only reason apart from—' He stopped abruptly. After a pause he went on, 'He can't be pushed around, Pippa, and you know it.'

'Oh, yes, I know it,' she said bitterly, 'but what can I do? We have to get out. Rena has practically said so. What *can* I do, Crag?'

'I told you,' was his reply.

'But I . . . but you . . .'

'You said that before and I agreed with you that we

don't. But what I offer still makes sense, girl, in fact it's the only thing that does make sense. For all of us.'

'All of us?'

'Davy, who would break his heart if you took him away, and you know it.'

'Yes' ... a little angrily ... 'I know it. You should never have let the association between you build up to this.'

'Well,' he shrugged, 'it has. Then me, Pippa, I want the boy. I want him very much.'

'That instant family?'

'Yes ... yet just for Davy himself as well. I love the little scrubber. Finally, you.'

'Yes. Where do I come in, why is it the only thing for me?'

'Because what makes Davy happy must make you contented, because you're dedicated to Davy, because Davy—'

'But what about *me*?' She was surprised at the sudden note in her voice. She was surprised at what she had said.

He had leaned nearer to her, and instinctively she drew back.

'Well, what about you, Pippa?' he asked softly.

'I ... I ...'

'Yes, girl?'

'I ... You're right, of course. It's only Davy who matters.' She spoke calmly, and it was difficult with such a sudden fast beating heart. 'But, Crag,' she added, 'does it have to be – marriage?'

'What else?'

'Well, I could go as your housekeeper,' she suggested.

'Not up there. It's a funny thing, Pippa' ... he was attending his pipe now ... 'it's a primitive corner all right, but not in that. Also, the way I feel about the scrubber it just wouldn't work. No, girl, that boy has to belong.'

'But you'd be saddling yourself, can't you see that?'

'I reckon if a horse is saddled the right way he's just as happy and a deal more secure than running free. I've actually seen it, Pippa, I've seen it up there.'

'Up there,' she said thoughtfully. 'I can't believe it's formal as you say, I can't believe I could not go merely as your housekeeper.'

'I have one already and she's not leaving,' he replied calmly. 'Besides that, there's the trip up. You see we'd be going overland. Camping out.'

'Camping out? But Davy—'

'Would thrive on it. I'm sure of that. I know he would benefit from those outback nights.'

'It still doesn't comprise a real reason for you to – to saddle yourself,' she said.

'One tent,' he answered levelly, 'you, the scrubber and me. It's a long way up, and you don't clutter yourself with gear.'

She had reddened, but she still held out.

'You would be cluttering yourself, Crag, can't you see that? – a sick boy, his sister.'

'My son,' he corrected soberly, 'my wife.'

'Oh, Crag, stop it! I – I can't be your wife.'

'If you're meaning what I think you're meaning I'll take you on those conditions as well,' he said quietly.

She flushed even more vividly, understanding him, then shook her head.

'I'm not a child,' she said gravely. 'I realize that complying to a certain state means more than living as – well, as I lived before.'

'I just told you if you want to make conditions, I'll accept you on them.'

'And keep to the conditions after the acceptance?'

He did not answer for a long moment, then he said, 'I don't know, Pippa. I feel like saying "Until you say", but—' He made a gesture with his big shoulders.

'Why did you make the offer in the first place?' she demanded.

'Because, dammit, I want to marry you,' he came back, 'because I want to have the scrubber with me, because that housekeeping thing of yours would be no go. Now are you answered?'

'No.'

'Right, you're not answered, but will you agree?'

Drearily she said, 'What else is there? What else?'

'Does that mean yes?'

'Yes.'

'Then say it, girl!'

'I just said it.'

'Say it with something in it,' he demanded.

She thought of Davy and what this would mean to him. She repeated, '*Yes.*'

He leaned right forward now and he kissed her lips. She simply stopped there in the caress, and he released her and said, 'He's a nice little scrubber, but does he have to stand between?'

'What do you mean, Crag?'

He gave a dismissive shrug, then told her he would like to get away immediately.

'We can get married tomorrow, Pippa,' he announced.

'Tomorrow?' She was taken aback. 'That soon?'

'It's got to be soon. I have to get back to Falling Star before it falls down.'

'You could go on and we could come later.'

'I told you I wanted Davy to have this camping experience.'

'Then you and Davy . . .'

'*Us*, Pippa. Look, girl, can't you see what Rena will try next? No' . . . a little sigh . . . 'you don't see it, do you, you never did. Never mind, it won't matter once we get away. But we can't do that until you're Mrs. Crag, so I've told the local minister—'

'*What?*'

'Oh, yes, and Davy, too. He's tickled pink.'

'You told Davy?' She could hardly believe him. 'How could you tell him when you didn't know?'

'I told him,' he repeated. 'I reckoned he'd like to be there when it was done. I reckoned you'd want that.'

'I would want that, but – but – tomorrow,' she said incredulously again.

'Tomorrow, Pippa,' he nodded.

A silence descended. It stopped so long that Pippa found herself searching for something to break it.

She could find nothing . . . and into the void came his soft: 'Want to back out, Pippa?' then her own: 'No.'

'Right then, we're being married. In the town at ten in the morning. After that we push off.'

'Rena—' she began.

'You can tell her if you like, but it might be hard to find her. I saw her leave Uplands just before I came into the planting. She'll probably be gone for some time, I'd reckon, while she thinks things over.'

'Then I can't tell her,' realized Pippa, half relieved, half uncertain.

'No.'

'Then I . . . then we just leave?'

'A little matter of a ceremony first,' he reminded her wryly.

'It's – unbelievable,' she said wonderingly.

'For me as well,' he said quietly.

'Then, Crag, why are you—'

'No, Pippa, not again. Ten tomorrow. And if you're not

there—'

'Yes?'

But he did not tell her. He just touched her shoulder briefly, then turned away. The next moment in the thickness of the trees he was gone.

Back again at Uplands, Pippa found that what Crag had said was correct. Rena had left.

Mrs. Mallory, the housekeeper, and the only resident servant since the rest of the domestic staff came in daily, told Pippa that Miss Rena had come in, walked around restlessly, then, when she had asked her could she get her something, help her in any way, had replied, 'Yes, Mallie, throw some things in a bag for me, I'm going away for a while to think.'

'Then,' reported Mrs. Mallory to Pippa, 'she said an odd thing, she said "I don't suppose I'll be thrown out straight off".'

Briefly, Pippa enlightened her, after all she had to know some time.

'That explains her paying up the daily girls,' nodded Mrs. Mallory, 'telling me to take a break and she'd see me again when she returned.'

The housekeeper did not look very concerned for herself, and when Pippa timidly asked if leaving Uplands would inconvenience her, she smiled and said, 'I don't think it will come to that.'

'But, Mrs. Mallory, the will—'

'Oh, yes, the will. But I've known Miss Rena since she was a child.' A little smile. 'I've also known Mr. Hardy a few years.'

Pippa searched the housekeeper's face for a sign of what she was thinking, but Mrs. Mallory was not giving anything away.

'I would certainly like that break,' she said. 'Carter

could caretake for a week or so.' She looked hopefully at Pippa.

'Then why not?'

'I couldn't leave you, miss.'

'But I will be going myself tomorrow. I'm ... I'm ...' Pippa tried to frame the words: 'I'm being married.' They wouldn't come, though. It all seemed untrue. Surely it was untrue.

Fortunately Mrs. Mallory did not notice her awkwardness. She said eagerly, 'It's my sister, she's not at all well, and I'd like the opportunity of visiting her.'

'Then do so. Go now,' Pippa urged warmly.

'It would make a difference if I could get tonight's train. You see, my sister lives in a small town to which there's only a night connection. You'd be quite all right, Miss Bromley, Carter would be here. By the way, Miss Rena left a note.' The woman handed it to Pippa.

As Mrs. Mallory bustled out to gather her few things together, Pippa opened the envelope. The several lines were written hastily, and backed up the housekeeper's statement that Rena had left in a hurry.

'Sorry it's turned out like this, Pippa, but you know the reason. You're on your own feet now, as I am. Rena.'

She put the letter back and went in to see if she could assist Mrs. Mallory. 'Perhaps I could drive you to the station,' she offered.

'Miss Rena took her car.'

'The other car.'

'Carter had to follow her with it down to Mr. Hardy's office. I don't know why.'

But Pippa knew. And she could see Rena storming out of her own car, throwing down the keys of the car Carter had driven, throwing them at Dom and saying: 'Here it is. After all, it's yours.'

'Perhaps I could borrow the car from Mr. Hardy—' she

began.

'He's gone, too. He went soon after she did. But don't worry about a car, Miss Bromley, the bus goes into town to catch the train. Are you sure, miss, that you'll be all right?'

'Quite sure. Carter will be here, remember. Also, I can ring Mr. Crag. He . . . we . . .'

But Mrs. Mallory was anxious to go, so Pippa did not say it after all. She walked with the housekeeper to the gate and waited with her until the bus came.

On her way back she detoured around the barns and stables, but Dom was still absent. Carter, whom she met on her way back to the house, said he had left in a hurry . . . everyone was in a hurry . . . that Mr. Hardy had only paused long enough to tell Carter what to do.

'What if there's a birth?' she asked the man.

'He saw to that,' Carter assured her. 'No events for a week, miss.'

'I'll fix tea for us,' Pippa offered, but Carter said not to bother, he was going to a meeting in the village, and would eat in a friend's place.

'But don't be worried, Miss Bromley, I won't be late.'

'I'm not nervous,' Pippa assured him, and she went into the house and up to the bare room she had been allotted when she first came here, the room with the window that looked out on the incinerator and mulch heap.

She could have had any room she liked now, she thought without much interest. She wandered out into the hall, wondering what would become of the house. When the bell suddenly pealed, it startled her, and for a few moments she forgot to answer it, accustomed as she was to the staff attending to that.

The second peal awakened her, and she ran down the stairs. She wondered if it was Rena back again . . . Doctor Burt . . . Crag. But the head showing through the glass door was only a little head, and eagerly Pippa opened up and clasped Davy so tight in her arms, he promptly wriggled free.

'Sorry, darling,' she said.

He rubbed some of her crushes off, and announced, 'Crag sent me to sleep here tonight.' He looked at her anxiously. 'I have to ask something.'

'Yes, Davy?'

'I have to ask this.' Davy took an important breath, then said distinctly: 'Still agreed on it, mate?'

'Crag told you?'

'Yes.' The anxious look deepening.

'Agreed,' said Pippa, and at once the little face altered. Never, *never* had Pippa seen such sunshine in her small brother. She would not have credited he could be so glad. It fairly bubbled out of him, he could not contain himself, and somewhere in her, Pippa, too, knew a song. It's worth it, she thought, for Davy.

They had tea together in the kitchen, though very little was eaten. Davy looked about to burst ... and Pippa, though she prepared a dish, only played with the food when it was done.

'Crag said that.' Her brother frowned at her plate.

'You're as bad yourself,' she smiled.

'But one thing, you're to go to bed early.'

'Crag said that, too?'

'Yes, Pippa.'

'Well, I will. We both will.'

They did. Arm in arm they went to Davy's room, the beautifully appointed room that Rena had had arranged for him.

Davy went into his little bed, and Pippa lay down on the day bed ... where, to her surprise when she awakened in the morning, she actually went to sleep at once. She had thought she would lie awake, especially when tomorrow ...

But she slept. It was a long restful sleep. She opened her eyes to Davy handing her a not-too-hot cup of tea by its presence of leaves but looking so proud of himself that she drank it and declared it perfect.

He sat on the day bed beside her.

'Where's your wedding dress, Pippa?'

'Oh, darling, wedding dresses are for brides, I mean brides who are having big weddings and will be written up in the paper.'

'Then what are you wearing?'

'Oh, my brown, I suppose . . . or my grey wool.'

'Oh, Pippa!'

'But, darling . . .'

'Brides don't wear those things, they wear – they wear—'

'Veils. But it's different, Davy. Can't you see, darling, that I—'

'I didn't mean veils ezackly, I – I meant a colour not grey or brown. And I meant flowers, Pippa' . . . eagerly . . . 'flowers to carry. There's lots of flowers in the garden. I'm sure we could pick them. The gardener told me it was good to pick them sometimes.'

'Oh, yes, we could pick them, but—'

'Then let's, Pippa.'

What could she say? What could she say to that little eager face? Thank goodness it was a climate in which seasons made little difference and flowers were always available. Pulling on her dressing-gown, she went out with Davy and gathered enough white marguerites and early violets to form a posy. She tied them with blue ribbon to please the little boy, and after her shower she put on a short blue frock that toned with the violet and white, then tied a blue band round her hair.

'Pippa, you're a bride!' Davy beamed.

'You're a bride.'

Crag said it when she opened the door at ten minutes to ten at his ring.

'I did it for Davy,' she said quickly. 'I did it because—'

'Don't spoil it,' he said simply, and came right in. 'Got a buttonhole for me?'

She looked at him incredulously, and he nodded.

'The scrubber, too,' he said.

There were carnations in the garden, and she plucked two. While she fixed them into buttonhole order, Crag packed their suitcases into the waggon. The waggon was pulling a trailer, she noticed, and the trailer was packed high with camping gear. Already Davy was capering around the gear, but he came running back to be buttonholed.

'It's all so absurd,' Pippa began to complain of the carnation in the little boy's lapel, but she didn't get it out, for all at once it didn't seem absurd, it seemed – right. It was Davy's bliss, she supposed, but it was right.

She had meant to write a brief note to Rena, telling her what she had done, where she had gone.

It was only when she was entering the church that she remembered she had not done so. She told herself she must get Crag to drive her back to do it before they left on their— Before they left. Heavens, she had nearly thought honeymoon. She gave a nervous half-laugh.

Then she stifled the laugh and looked at the minister who had come to meet and to guide them. She heard him say to the three of them, Crag, Davy, herself . . . and to a cleaner, a gardener and someone brought in from the street:

'Dearly beloved, we are gathered together here in the sight of God and in the face of this congregation, to join together this man and this woman in Holy Matrimony.'

It was too late to go back. In that moment she realized it. But with the realization came another realization, a realization so big, so bewildering, that for a moment she swayed, and Crag put out a hand to steady her.

She did not want to go back. *She wanted this.*

She heard 'man and wife' ... she felt Crag's lips brushing hers. She felt Davy's younger lips. She felt the press of the minister's hand.

It was not until they were miles from the Southern Highlands that she recalled again the letter she had *not* written to Rena. She told Crag and he shrugged, 'Too late now, Mrs. C.'

Mrs. C. She was Mrs. C.

Beside her Davy chuckled delightedly and experimented, 'Pippa C. Mrs. C.' Then in a satisfied voice he said: 'My sister, Mrs. C.'

He was still smiling over it when he fell asleep somewhere on the road to Orange ... they were heading inland and hoping to make Bourke that night.

Pippa removed the carnation which he had refused to take from his lapel, and pressed his little head to her shoulder. The carnation was wilted and crushed and she went to throw it away ... and then she didn't. Instead she put it in her bag.

'Mine, too.' Crag took out his and handed it to her, and for a moment their eyes met.

Then he turned his attention on the road again. By nightfall they reached Bourke.

CHAPTER SIX

'BOURKE isn't just a western town,' Crag said as they left the main street, 'it's a last stand before the hinterland sets in. Songs have been sung about it, verses written. Everyone speaks of "Out at the back-o'-Bourke".'

'How far back are we going, Crag?' Davy, who had wakened up, asked eagerly.

'As back as Falling Star finally, scrubber, but right now only a mile back to the river where I reckon we'll make camp.'

An uncertainty enveloped Pippa. She had enjoyed her journey, finding the country much more as she had imagined Australia, not the second England the green Highlands had proved.

But making camp meant her first night as a wife. What had the man beside her said? One tent. You, the scrubber and me.

If Pippa was uncertain, though, Davy was rapturous. He was out of the waggon as soon as they reached the camping ground, helping Crag choose a suitable site, making ponderous agreements as to drainage should it rain . . . rain with a sky of flawless satin! . . . shelter should it blow . . . with not even a breath to stir the starlit leaves of the trees by which they would pitch the tent! *One* tent.

Crag decided on the most suitable spot, then set Davy to gather fuel and tinder. From now on that would be his duty, Crag informed him, until they reached Falling Star.

Pippa's duty, he said next, would be to start the tucker. Pippa nodded, and began laying the chops on the grid he had set out, but at once she was told to wait for the embers, since cooking over that flame would smoke the meat. Again Pippa nodded.

While Davy gathered the fuel, then threw it on ... Pippa was a little nervous about that, but Crag appeared to have confidence in the boy, so she must, too ... and while she waited, Crag pitched the tent and unrolled the sleeping bags. Then he came back to the fire and gave Pippa her first lesson in damper.

'I can make soda bread,' she said a little stiffly, 'which is the same.'

'No soda in this,' he instructed. 'Ashes.'

'Ashes!'

'Potash is a form of rising.' He took some from the spent end of the fire. 'You take your flour, salt and a handful of ashes and some water. Then you knead.' He did so. He told her to put the chops on the grid now and to stand by to turn them, then he finished his kneading and pushed the damper well in, saying it would be awaiting them for their breakfast.

They ate under a deep blue cloth of sky, the stars glittering with a brilliance never seen on the coast, Crag claimed.

Then, replete and drowsy, they all agreed on bed. While Crag built up the fire for the night, Pippa undressed the little boy down to his singlet and underpants and slipped him into the bag.

'God bless,' she kissed.

'Am I next?' Crag drawled as she came outside again. He was sitting near the tent flap and smoking his eternal pipe.

'I'll say God bless to you,' she promised lightly.

'Also tuck me in the bag?'

She flushed in the darkness, and reminded him, 'You'd be more of a job than Davy.'

He did not comment on that, he tended his pipe, and she stared out at the velvet darkness beyond the fire's flickering beams. A little noise that rose above the soft stir of the bush and the ripple of the river alerted her, but Crag assured her it was only a pheasant on the forage.

'He says "puss-puss",' he told her. 'Listen.'

Soon afterwards there was another bush noise that Crag said would be a wood pigeon.

'He calls "move-over-dear".' A laugh. 'Not much good in a sleeping bag, would you say, Mrs. C.?'

Davy gave a little possum snore, and Pippa went rather thankfully in to see to him . . . and to slip into her own niche.

She was drifting off when Crag finally came to his sleeping bag. He was so quiet she might not have known, except that he came across to her and kissed her cheek.

'Good night, Mrs. C.'

Now wide awake and staring into the darkness where he must be but she couldn't see him, Pippa answered a little indistinctly, 'God bless.'

The next morning the damper was taken from the white embers, its casing sliced off to reveal a perfect soda . . . no, potash, remembered Pippa . . . loaf that was deliciously warm enough to send the butter that Crag knifed generously over it into golden runnels.

'Mmm!' said Davy, eating more than Pippa had ever seen him eat. His little chin dripped runnels of gold.

Crag brewed tea, throwing the leaves into the boiling water, rotating the billy bush-style, and they drank and listened to the river and the sound of the awakening bush.

They set off again after Crag had carefully doused the fire, instructing Davy meanwhile how very important this was. Then he cleaned up the site to make it attractive for the next campers, telling Davy about this, too. Pippa saw

Davy nodding as he absorbed every word.

Now they went west, the bush road as straight as a gun barrel, and the names rolled from Crag's tongue ... Milparinka, Tibooburra, Wittabrinna, Wompah. On the rim of Carya-punda Swamp they crossed the Queensland border.

Camp that night was by an overflow, and the sounds of the water birds enchanted Pippa as she helped Davy gather the fuel, which, because the trees had become sparse, was not so easy to find as at Back-o'-Bourke. Crag had told her to delay the meal until he went up to a station he knew. But, the fire started and thriving, Pippa could not resist trying a damper herself. Davy looked a little dubiously at the rather darkish result and asked his sister was she sure she had used white ashes.

'Yes.' Indignantly.

'Then it must be your hands.'

'It'll be all right. You'll see in the morning.' She shoved the damper in, Davy still looking dubious.

But at that moment the waggon came back, and Crag jumped out and held up three huge steaks. 'Also,' he rejoiced, 'station bread.' He exhibited a crusty loaf.

'I've already put in a damper,' Pippa informed him loftily.

'Good for you. But just in case ...'

Pippa tossed her head at that 'just in case'.

There was also fresh milk for Davy, and a bottle of home preserves. By the time of the billy routine that finished off the meal three people were well fed and three heads were nodding.

Pippa was first up in the morning, and she went stealthily to the spent fire. She poked around ... and poked around. There was no damper.

Crag came to the flap of the tent, let her search for a while, then drawled, 'Were you looking for a cricket ball,

119

by any chance?'

'No, of course not, I was looking for a—' She saw the laughter in his face, and stopped. After a few moments of private wrath, she accused, 'That's not funny!'

'Neither was the ball, brick, what-have-you.'

'It was soda . . . I mean potash bread.'

'Leave out the bread,' he advised with a grin, 'for that's all there was, a ball of baked ash. Knowing small boys, and how they love to tease, I removed the evidence, Mrs. C.'

'I'm not!' she cried angrily, for she really had looked forward to surprising him with that damper.

'No.' His voice cut in quietly but all the more intensive because of its quietness. 'No, you're not, are you?'

She flushed vividly, suddenly aware of his bright eyes on her. 'I meant I'm Mrs. Crag, not that ridiculous Mrs. C.'

There was a pause. In the silence Pippa could hear Davy stirring. She knew she should go into the tent and help the little boy out of his bag, for he had the knack of tangling himself up. But somehow she could not pass Crag in that narrow space he had left her.

The silence grew. Even Davy did not break it again, so he must have gone back to sleep.

Then Crag broke it. He said: 'I wasn't meaning that.' He still looked at her, until, with an effort, she brushed past him into the tent.

Davy remembered the damper. Munching on a steak sandwich, he related the damper to Crag, and how Pippa had either used black ashes or her hands had given it a funny colour.

'Didn't turn out funny, though,' said Crag. 'Sorry I didn't leave you any, scrubber, but I was so hungry when I woke up last night—'

'You ate it all?' Davy did not look so much regretful as

incredulous, incredulous that anyone could have demolished that brick. He dropped the subject, though, for which Pippa knew she should be grateful to Crag. She was not. All the same she tossed him a cold appreciation of his lie.

'Needn't have been a lie,' he grinned. 'I was up last night, listening to the frog song down in the Overflow, looking up at the stars.'

All at once she pictured it . . . the velvet night, the star shadows, the bright moon, the crooning whispers and the soft rustling of the bush.

She wished she had been there, too.

'Why don't you, Pippa? Why don't you come?' He said it as though she had spoken her thoughts aloud. She jumped to her feet, aware of her scarlet cheeks, and began getting ready for the road again.

'Tomorrow,' Crag told Davy, 'you'll be wearing a fly veil.'

'Why, Crag?'

'For flies, of course. They're not everywhere Inside, but they are where we'll be passing through. Bush flies.'

'How will we eat, Crag? Through the holes?'

'If you intend eating only currants, yes, scrubber, but I think you can sneak in a mouthful here and there, then at night they'll be gone, they don't care about fire.'

'Where will we be?'

'Latitude twenty, I'd say.'

'What does that mean, Crag?' Pippa heard Davy's little voice as her brother followed his idol down to the water to get replenishment for the radiator. She heard Crag's patient answer. He was good father-material, she thought, and with that thought came a regret for him that so far that had been denied.

So far. . . . She stopped what she was doing. Although she had said to the man who was now her husband: 'I'm not a child. I realize that complying to a certain state means more than living as I lived before,' she had never really thought about it. Now she thought.

'All aboard!' called Crag, and they were on their way again.

Each day, each moment of the day, the country changed. They were in the Inside now, that strange, unpredictable hinterland where for hundreds of miles there was nothing but red sand and gibber, saltpans, claypans, dry inland seas, but where at times, without warning, a blossoming burst on you, a verdure so intense that it hurt the eyes, flowers of unbelievable size and the tenderest of hues.

When Pippa called out that the paradise she suddenly looked out on must be a mirage, Crag shook his head, then told her that out here mirages came in different wrappings from the usual mirages . . . for instance drivers of trailers saw opposite trailers drawn up on the wrong side of the road, often they swerved to avoid them coming at them.

'Fatigue?' asked Pippa.

Crag shrugged. 'Perhaps . . . or a sort of second vision, a reflection. Look at that sign.' He pointed to a 'Beware of road trains 140 feet long'. Beside it a warning: 'No water for 900 miles.'

'Have we enough?'

'I know the wurlies around here – a wurlie is an old aboriginal watering hole. Also if you can teach yourself the plastic trick to trap moisture you won't parch. This is it . . .'

Davy was breathing down his neck in intrigue, and Pippa realized she was doing almost the same. This strange fascinating desert!

The red ochre days continued, the lupin-blue ridges that at night turned indigo, purple and scarlet. They passed a buffalo herd being headed in by buffalo hunters wearing ten-gallon hats against a blazing sun. These beasts were to be shipped to Singapore to work, and strangely it was from Singapore originally that they had come to work here. They passed camels, donkeys, packs of dingoes, flocks of galahs, graceful brolgas.

Now the nights were wine-dark until the moon came up, but before that Crag always made camp.

'Two fingers above the horizon,' he told Davy, 'is enough travelling for the day.' He held his big hand side-wise, extending two fingers.

'Your fingers or mine, Crag?' asked Davy.

'I see what you mean, scrubber. We'll make it yours this time and camp here.' As he drew up the waggon, he said: 'This is the last night's camp, folk.'

'What?' Pippa turned in surprise to him, but only Pippa, so Davy must have known already, but then there was little of this trip and this country that that young fellow did not know.

'Tomorrow,' nodded Crag, 'is Falling Star.'

It was with an odd feeling of the end of something in her life, almost the final turning of a page denoting a book is finished, that Pippa prepared the meal that night.

Davy was in high spirits, gathering tinder and fuel with nervous energy, anticipating what tomorrow would bring.

What *would* tomorrow bring? Pippa stared at the fire gathering embers much more quickly surely than it generally gathered them, forming white ashes for the damper ... she was expert on that now ... making the end of a day come faster. – And the beginning of a night.

She was silent as she ate that evening, silent later as she tucked Davy into his bag. She stopped with him long after her 'God bless', long after his little possum snores

123

told her that he slept. At length she knew she could stop no longer, yet still she lingered. There was a pulse and a throb in her that she had never known before. It was with an effort that she lifted the flap of the tent and went outside.

Crag was sitting out of the beam of the fire, for it was warm up here, no need to hug the glowing embers. She could just see his big dark outline against a tree.

He saw her, though. He got up. 'I was waiting for you,' he called ... and as though impelled there she went across.

For a moment they stood looking at each other, then he took her in his arms, and she did not resist.

The navy blue night encompassed them. The stars. A silver of moon. Somewhere the pheasant cried out its 'Puss-puss', the wood pigeon began its 'Move-over-dear'. He ... Crag ... had smiled that that would be hard in a sleeping bag.

But they were not in sleeping bags now, they were on soft earth, and a tree leaned over.

'Good night, Mrs. Crag,' Crag called as he got into his sleeping bag in the tent, but she pretended oblivion at once, and did not answer.

For I am, she knew now. I am Mrs. Crag, not Mrs. C.

I am Crag's wife.

Every moment of that final day brought Pippa a mounting excitement. Always she had thought of her stay at Falling Star as something temporary, merely a waiting until Davy ...

Never had she thought of the place which they would reach at sundown ... Crag, veering north-west now, had just reported that ... as home. It wasn't, either. It was just a pause for her, a pause only, and yet . . .

She looked out on the nothingness either side, an astonishing nothingness, for the longer you gazed at it the more features . . . and *beauty* . . . it achieved, and wished she could lose this foolish concept of journey's end. For Yantumara could never be her journey's end. It was the scrubber that man loved . . . there, she was calling him that herself now . . . and because of that love he had married her. Just to have Davy. Last night . . . her cheeks flamed . . . had only been part of the biological pattern of life. Life went on. People went on. Children. What if— The sudden thought caught her breath. Oh, no, it wouldn't happen: Yet what if it did? She gave the man at her side an oblique glance. How had she thought of him? As good father-material. What if . . .

When the sun was right above them, Crag pulled up for lunch. While Davy examined one of the giant anthills that were part of the scene now, Crag, boiling a billy so quickly with dry tinder he almost could have pulled on an electric switch, said wryly: 'Relax, Pippa.'

'Relax?' She gave a start, then looked at him in question.

'There are eight rooms at Falling Star.' He threw on more tinder. 'Five of them bedrooms. We' . . . a deliberate pause . . . 'will only be using two.'

'Two?' she queried.

'The scrubber and I in one so I can watch him and you can stop wearing yourself out, another for you. No' . . . as she went to intervene . . . 'I know what you're going to say. You're going to tell me like you did before that complying to a certain state . . . stop me if I use the wrong words . . . means more than living as you lived before.'

'Crag,' she said awkwardly, 'I want to be fair.'

'Fair?' He repeated the word incredulously. He almost seemed to try out its taste. 'Fair?'

'Crag, I . . . I . . .'

'Look, Pippa.' He looked up at her from his squatting position, the tinder dangling from his big hand. 'Look, girl, last night didn't establish anything. I mean there's no ties tied. I mean—'

'Yes, Crag, what do you mean?'

'That it was nothing. *Now* relax.'

Relax. Pippa turned away.

Davy had run back from the anthills full of questions. The man answered him as to their magnetic properties as he scattered the tea-leaves in the bubbling water, then rotated the billy.

'Not much for tucker,' he regretted, 'but tonight will be better. I telephoned Mrs. Cassidy at the last station.'

'Who is Mrs. Cassidy?' Pippa asked.

'My housekeeper, and my father's before me. That's why you couldn't have taken over that role, girl.'

'Won't Mrs. Cassidy feel it's odd that we . . . I mean . . .' She glanced towards Davy, but he was still pondering over the anthills.

'She's had scrubbers of her own,' said Crag, 'and she'll accept that a man sometimes needs a man's attention. Anyway' . . . he poured three teas . . . 'she lives in her own cottage.'

'A cottage as well as the homestead?'

'It's practically a little town. Most of the Inside places have to be that. They form their own world. When you're hundreds of miles from a store you start your own store. That applies to amusements, too. For instance, you show your own movies.'

'Do you, Crag?' asked Davy enchanted, forgetting the anthills.

'Sure do, scrubber. You have your own church, your own sick bay, all the things an ordinary town would have.'

'Doctor?' said Pippa in a low voice.

He understood her concern. 'No, I don't take over that side, unless of course it's an emergency until the F.D. can get in.'

'F.D.?'

'Flying Doctor. Though I do dole out physic when needed to the pics.'

'Piccaninnies.'

'Yes. The scrubber won't lack young friends, Pippa.' At her frown he said stoutly, 'They're lovely youngsters, Davy will do himself proud.'

'Of course,' Pippa assured him, 'it was the lack of a medico that was concerning me. I mean if suddenly . . .' Her glance went to Davy.

'Then just as quick as down south we get aid. Quicker, I'd reckon, there's no traffic in the sky, so that the F.D. or F.A.—'

'F.A.?' asked Pippa now.

'Flying Ambulance, ready to take a patient to the nearest base hospital, or, if more than that is needed, even down to Sydney or Melbourne. I tell you, girl, you've no worries.'

'No,' she said, relieved.

During the afternoon's ride some occasional green crept into the red earth and rocks, and Crag said that around here was cotton country.

'There's water, you see, something a cotton stand must have.'

'Haven't you water?'

'Cattle amount. Cotton needs more.' He had pulled up the waggon for her to see the plants at nearer range. She found the shrubs in bloom very pretty, even bridal.

'Why not when we have a bride here?' he teased. 'Along the track is the ginnery. I'll take you there one day.'

Soon the green cut out and the mulga and spinifex began again, the bare bones of rocks. They circled an emu's nest so as not to disturb the mother. Later on there was another detour around a taboo ground, a place, Crag explained, where the natives believed ancestors walked.

Davy did not sleep during the long warm afternoon, his eyes were wide.

'What will happen, Crag,' he asked, 'if the sun gets down to two fingers and we're still not at Falling Star?'

'I reckon we'd push on, scrubber. I know the track like the back of my hand. Only it's not going to happen. See that hill?'

By this both Davy and Pippa had begun really to see hills in Crag's 'hills'. At first they had laughed at them, refusing to admit even a slight rise when he had pointed out Mount Westward ... Purple Mountain ... Gully Peak ... The Ramparts ... But now they had adjusted their ideas ... and their vision ... and they both called eagerly, 'Yes.'

'Beyond that is Falling Star. In half a finger more, Davy, you'll be looking at your home.'

'Oh!' Davy breathed, and he judged the westering sun by his little digit held sidewise. Presently he called, 'The sun has moved that half finger, Crag.'

'And Yantumara awaits.'

'Where? I can't see.... Oh, yes.'

Pippa, too, had focused the setting. With Davy she sat silent while the waggon gathered speed on familiar ground and the distant cluster of buildings became more distinct.

'It's a township,' Pippa called.

'Not really,' Crag grinned.

'But all those buildings—'

'The land has been good to the Crags, and that in-cludes those who lived on our land, so we've given back

what we can. Those cottages' ... he waved his hand ...
'replace the humpies of my grandfather's day. That shed
is an amenities hall, that small building our little hospital.
There's Mrs. Cassidy's happy home. Next door is the
book-keeper, and then there's a dormitory for the stockmen. And that's—'

Davy finished for him in a reverent voice: 'Falling
Star.'

'Yantumara,' nodded Crag. He had slackened speed so
that he could gaze, too, at his home.

Pippa saw that Ku, as he had told her, had copied its
pattern, there was the same sprawling design at Ku, the
same wide verandahs. But the setting here, she smiled to
herself, was very different. No cool country lushness at
Yantumara, no singing pines, just the bare hot hinterland. Yet there was a tree ... a rather strange speci-
men.

'It's a baobob,' said Crag, starting off again to finish the
last short lap, 'a bottle tree. Folk have been known actually to live in that wide trunk, but we're not going to.
Stand aside, scrubber.' He had halted now and lifted
them both out. 'This is something I'm told has to be
done.'

As he approached her Pippa saw what he intended to
do, and she said half in vexation and half in laughter,
'Oh, don't be silly, Crag.'

'Don't you be silly. I couldn't do it before, I couldn't
carry you over the threshold of a tent.' As he spoke he
lifted her in his arms and bore her through the open door,
Davy dancing delightedly at his heels, an audience of
little dark people ... and quite a few not so little ... at the
foot of the verandah. Also some ten-gallon hat men,
stockmen probably, a man with a ledger under his arm,
he would be the book-keeper, a woman in an apron, she
would be Mrs. Cassidy. Others.

'Oh, put me down,' Pippa implored.

He did . . . in a room that at once enchanted Pippa. It was large, with a cool cemented floor that had been painted green and polished to a high gloss. The blinds were rattan, the furniture bamboo, everything was for coolness, except the fireplace where fires would never be lit, and there, very effectively, either Mrs. Cassidy or the girls had arranged dried feathers of long grass.

Crag, watching her closely and seeing her approval, remarked of the fireplace, 'I told you that my great-greats only thought in terms of so many rooms and as many chimneys.'

'I like it,' she assured him.

Davy was scampering around the house, discovering it all for himself, occasionally letting out squeals of joy.

'There's a sea outside, Pippa. Look through the window!'

'Lagoon,' called Crag. 'We've had some wet. It mightn't be there next month.'

'There's a windmill and a corral.'

'We usually say pen, scrubber. Pippa, meet Cass, the best dab sponge hand Up Top. Cass, this is—'

'I'm glad to meet your wife, Crag,' the older woman greeted Pippa warmly. 'Your mother would have loved to have seen this day.'

Your wife. All through the tea that Mrs. Cassidy insisted on serving at once, even though the main meal could not be far away, Pippa kept on hearing those two words. Your wife.

The tea over, Mrs. Cassidy now insisted on running across to her own place while Pippa got her bearings. She would be back to serve the dinner, she said.

There was a sensitiveness in this back-country woman, Pippa saw, and she warmed to her. She wanted to say: 'Don't go. It doesn't matter. You see – this is a different marriage.'

Then Crag was taking her along to her room, showing her the larger room he would share with Davy.

'Tonight we'll go through things, medical things concerning the scrubber,' he said, 'you'll tell me what to watch for in Davy.'

'He's my responsibility,' protested Pippa.

He patted her shoulder. 'Why don't you flake out until dinner? Incidentally Mrs. Cass always does the cooking. Up till now I've eaten with the men, and I thought it might interest Davy if we continued doing so. Suit you?'

'Of course. Unless—'

'Yes?'

'Unless you feel I should form a family table. I mean—'

'You mean you at one end, me at the other, the scrubber in between? Compliance to a certain state?'

'Oh, Crag!' she said almost tearfully.

At once he was contrite. He touched her head gently, said, 'Rest now,' and left.

But after he had gone she sat broodingly at the window, not looking at the new fresh things that at first had captured her attention, thinking wretchedly instead of this big warm house, and what this house should be. — What this house wasn't.

It should be filled with love ... and the children who come from that love. Of course there was the love of Davy, but for how long? How much more borrowed time?

She stared through the window but did not see the faintly mauve-grey grass that turned iridescent every time the small breeze teased at its blades, she did not see the glittering lagoon. When a bell went for dinner ... she supposed it would be dinner, for no one would 'dress' here

. . . she had only time to dab her eyes before Crag knocked and called 'Tucker!'

If he noticed pink rims he said nothing, but he did appeal before he opened the dining-room door an anxious: 'They're looking forward to you, Pippa, you're the only woman, bar Mrs. Cass, whom they see every day, for five hundred miles.'

'You're asking me to smile.' She did smile.

'Thanks, girl.' He turned the handle and pushed the door.

There was one long table with benches each side, and everyone sat there. That is they did until she entered, then they rose while Crag introduced them all to her.

'Barney, Snowy, Harry, Nobby,' said Crag. 'Boys, the Missus.'

Four leather-dark faces creased into smiles, and the eyes, deep in the creases from years in the sun, disappeared.

'Rupey, our bookie.' Rupert took off his glasses and bowed.

'Tim and Tom, two helpful jackeroos,' put in one of a pair of fresh-faced boys.

'Hopeful of stopping on considering the mistakes they've made while I've been away,' growled Crag, and the other half of the pair retorted that it could be hopeful of getting out of here, but his voice did not back up what he said.

There were others, sundry helpers, Pippa judged, and they all smiled appreciatively at her, so much so that tomorrow she resolved to wear a pretty dress and have bright eyes.

Davy's eyes, however, were positively glistening. Not from the company, she soon found out, and not from the festive board, but from the audience at the window. There was literally a score of little dark heads and double that of pansy eyes staring at Davy. Davy, who had known few contemporaries because of his restricted existence, looked back at them in fascination.

At last he could bear it no longer, and he tugged at Crag.

'Crag, where do they eat?'

'In their own houses, of course, scrubber, like you're eating ... or I expect you to start soon.' He picked up Davy's knife and fork to prompt him. 'Only,' Crag continued, 'mainly their mums make one big fire and cook the rib bones there together.'

'Rib bones?'

'Over a eucalyptus fire there's nothing better.'

'Oh.' Davy looked with disappointment at his own tasteful plate.

'Look,' said Crag, 'if you lick that clean, tomorrow night you can have rib bones down there.'

Pippa gave a little gasp, and Crag said, 'Won't do any harm, in fact a power of good. I grew up on meals like that.'

'But Davy's different,' she said in a low voice. 'You shouldn't tell him things that will leave him disappointed.'

'Rib bones never disappointed anyone.'

'You know I didn't mean that,' she said angrily.

'Smile,' he advised. 'Only woman, save Cass, for five hundred miles, remember.'

Pippa, feeling more like kicking his shins, smiled.

Davy, prompted by Crag's promise, reassured by the shy welcomes on the little brown faces at the window, ate his meal, listening with fascination to the station talk of herds, horse-breaks, overlanding ... places called strange names like The Overtake, Big Dry, Come And Get It.

It appeared that a horse-break was going on this week. The wild horses had been rounded up last month and

133

now there was the job of breaking them in. The mares had been done, said one of the stockmen in a soft voice that rather surprised Pippa for a man in such a tough position, and they had been nervous but easy enough, but the stallions had been a challenge.

'Especially,' came in the stockman Harry in an equally soft tone, 'that older feller we haven't got round to yet. He promises to be a bad 'un.'

Mrs. Cass brought out plum duff . . . she was certainly a great cook . . . then all took their plates and scraped them and placed them in a dishwasher and poured their tea from a huge brown pot.

The little pansy-eyed people had faded away from the window – no doubt, explained Pippa to Davy, they had gone to bed. On hearing this, Davy, too, agreed on bed, and Pippa took him along to the room he was to share with Crag.

'It will be funny,' said the now experienced Davy, 'sleeping under a roof.'

'You liked the tent better, darling?' Pippa was fixing a pillow.

'Oh, no,' Davy assured her, 'I like it here, it's my home.'

My home. He said it with such faith and assurance, Pippa's eyes pricked. How long a home?

'I feel like crying for joy, too, Pip.' Davy, mistaking her tears, smiled it up at her. He said proudly, proud of himself, 'You can go now. I don't need you to sit with me while I go to sleep, not any more.' As she rose obediently and went to the door, he called, 'Pippa, you'll tell him, won't you?'

'Tell whom, darling? Tell what?'

'Tell your husband about me not needing you to sit with me.'

'Yes, I will, Davy.'

'And Pippa—'

'Yes, Davy?'

'Tell him I think that very soon I won't want anyone ever at all. Will you tell him?'

'Yes, Davy.' She went slowly out. No one ever at all. Davy had said it with pride, he had always been sharply conscious of his dependence. But she had not heard it with pride but misery, because there soon would be . . . no one ever at all.

No more springs. Doctor Harries had told her that, and already that last spring was three months gone.

She found her way to the big room where she expected, by its lights, Crag would be awaiting her. The stockmen, the book-keeper, jackeroos and general helpers had departed to their own quarters. Mrs. Cassidy's kitchen light was out, so she must have left, too.

Pippa knocked on the door, then entered the cool domain. Crag got up from the bamboo rocker he was relaxing in and insisted she take it.

'No,' he said as she objected to shifting him out, 'I like seeing a woman rock, it looks more in keeping than a man rocking.'

'I think a man is more in keeping,' she argued, 'a man sitting on a porch smoking his pipe and looking back through the years.'

'Do I seem that old to you?' he grinned.

'No, it's just how I see a man and a rocker.'

'Shall I tell you how I see a woman and a rocker? I see her there with a baby and singing lullabies.'

'I suppose your mother rocked you here,' said Pippa a little stiffly, 'sang you lullabies.' Before he could elaborate, she prompted, 'You wanted to talk to me about Davy.'

'Yes.' He waited to light his pipe.

As he did so, Pippa remarked on the stockmen and how

impressed she had been that such big tough fellows could speak in such gentle, controlled voices.

He put down his pipe at that and laughed till the tears came down his cheeks.

'Barney, Snowy, Harry, Nobby,' he guffawed. 'Gentle, controlled voices! Wait till I tell the jackeroos.'

'I don't see anything funny.'

'You'll hear it, though, when I take you out to see a muster. Of course the fellers' voices are gentle and controlled, they're saving them for the next time they're cracking a whip and digging in the spurs as they take off after a trouble-maker. But' ... seeing that Pippa was still unamused ... 'it's nice of you to tag them "gentle and controlled".'

'Don't you like your staff?'

'Like them?' He looked at her amazed.

'You don't sound as though you do. Though perhaps' ... coolly ... 'you dislike anything gentle and controlled.'

He did not answer for quite a while. Then he said in a rather husky voice: 'It's not always easy to be that. Gentle and controlled.' He had got up and gone to the window. She saw that the knuckles of the hands on the sill were strained and white. 'Not easy,' he said again.

There was a long pause. Feeling uncomfortable, yet not understanding why, Pippa reminded him what they had come together to talk about. He nodded and came back to sit beside her, and then quietly but firmly he drew from her every detail she could give him concerning Davy. The first grave signs in a small child, the attention he had been given since, what each doctor of the many doctors had reported. Finally Doctor Burt.

'Glen Burt repeated what I had previously learned, but he said that every day new reading was coming in concerning Davy's trouble. He said—'

'Yes, Pippa?'

'That sometimes in spite of facts, in spite of all a doctor knows, it doesn't always happen as a doctor believes. But' . . . a break now in Pippa's voice . . . 'how long can a little boy wait?'

Several times during the long questioning Crag got up and made tea. Then he would come back and ask for more. But finally the questions stopped, and they sat silent in a room that Pippa realized with drowsy surprise was fast becoming lighter. They had talked all night.

Crag had got to his feet again, but this time not for tea. Leaning over, he gathered her up and carried her to her room. 'At least,' he said, 'you'll get an hour before early cuppa. – Though a fine watchdog I made for our scrubber.'

'You had to understand everything,' she defended for him, and knew it was the first defence she had made for Crag.

'Yes,' he agreed, 'and it was better to talk the night out than sit and think.'

She looked quickly at him, and he went on.

'*Think*,' he said, 'like you were thinking this afternoon, Pippa. Sitting at a window and thinking about this house.'

'How could you know—' she blurted, her cheeks burning. Then she stopped and looked away.

But he answered her unfinished question. He said, 'Because *I* was sitting at a window, too, thinking of what a house should be, but isn't. Grieving for a house. So it was better to talk out tonight, wasn't it? Though' . . . putting her down on the bed . . . 'it will be different . . . when a house *is*.'

CHAPTER SEVEN

WHEN a house *is*.

Pippa slept at last with those four words ringing in her mind. When a house is not a place of rooms but a place of love, she interpreted, but how could he ask love of her when the only love he offered was for her brother? Apart from Davy any woman could have stood where she stood. He had told her that first day on the train that time too soon ran out for life as life should be lived. Rena had set him back ... probably others ... so now it had finally come to Pippa Bromley. No. Pippa Crag.

'Missus,' said a soft voice, 'Missus,' and Pippa opened her eyes to a smiling girl with white teeth and coffee skin. 'Missus, you bin sleep long time. Missus Cass she sent me with cup of tea.'

Pippa started to explain that she had been asleep only a short time, but found she felt so refreshed that it was unnecessary. She smiled at the girl and said, 'Thank you—' with a question in her voice. The girl responded, 'Rosie.'

'It's very good of you, Rosie.' She took the tea.

'I'm kitchen girl,' beamed Rosie. 'I help Missus Cass. Your piccaninny 'e bin gone down with our pics.'

'Davy is up?'

'Dav-ee name belonga him? Yes, Missus. Your piccaninny, Missus?'

'My brother.'

'Oh.' Rosie looked sympathetic. 'Never mind, you have teetartaboo soon.'

'Teetartaboo?'

'Baby,' smiled Rosie. 'You and Boss have plenty babies.'

With pride she told Pippa, 'I have four.'

'Four!' She only looked a girl, though probably she had married in her early teens.

Pippa got up, gave her cup to Rosie, put on her dressing-gown and found the bathroom. The water ran very hot for a while and she remembered last night that Crag had told her there was no need for any heating system up here, the main concern was to run water cold. But eventually it gushed cooler and then quite cool. She finished off the shower with the cool and came back to her room braced and refreshed. She put on a simple shift, buckled up sandals, combed her hair and etched in a hint of lipstick, then went along to the kitchen.

Mrs. Cassidy was busy with more meat than Pippa had seen outside a butcher's shop.

'Up here we all kill our own, of course,' she told Pippa. 'Ben, he's our butcher, has just brought in today's meat to be dealt with.'

'All beef?'

'No lamb or mutton here, dear, it's steak, steak, steak.'

As Pippa gazed fascinated at the intimidating quantities of undercut, topside, chuck, sirloin and liver, Mrs. Cassidy said soothingly, 'Don't worry about it, you won't be called upon to deal with it. Unless' ... a quick inquiring glance at Pippa ... 'you want to. Crag's mother always left it to me, so naturally I thought you'd be the same. But I'm sure, Mrs. Crag, that if you wish—'

'I don't wish. I prefer things to go on as they went before. And I'm Pippa, Mrs. Cassidy.'

'Cass or Cassy will do nicely,' beamed the housekeeper, relieved to learn she still retained her position of kitchen boss. 'I like this work. You could say I was brought up to it. My mother was a station cook and used to bring me along with her. Old Mrs. Crag used to spend all her time on the piccaninnies, then her daughter-in-law, Crag's mother, did the same after her.'

Pippa nodded, but did not comment. *This* Crag woman won't, she thought hopelessly, because she won't be here long enough, only as long as Davy... Her throat contracted. She said a little huskily, 'I'd like to help in that way, too, but I have my brother, and unhappily—' Her voice trailed off.

The next moment she was surprised by two warm arms around her. 'There, lovie, it's going to be all right. I know all about it, Crag told me, so don't worry yourself trying to tell me now. And don't think as you've been thinking, either. Miracles happen. They happen every day.'

'I know, but can one happen soon enough?'

'I see what you mean. Well, let me tell you something: this is the land of lots o' time ... songs have been written about that. So I reckon young Davy will have lots o' time, too, and while he's having it those miracles will catch up.'

'Oh, Mrs. Cassidy ... Cassy!' Tears were splashing down Pippa's cheeks, but they were happy tears. Already she felt almost cheerful.

'Sit down and get that breakfast into you, girl. That's one rule at Falling Star: a big breakfast. On a station like this, with mobs and herds always on the move in or out, you always make certain of at least the first meal of the day.'

'But that's big enough for three meals!' gasped Pippa at the sight of her laden plate, for it was surely the biggest steak she had ever seen.

'The boy got it into him,' pooh-poohed the housekeeper.

'Davy did?' Pippa looked incredulous. 'He's never eaten a proper breakfast in his life.'

'He did this time. Look, if you don't wrap yourself

around it, as Crag always says, I'll put another piece on.'

Laughing ... and hungrier than she had believed she was, especially after the first bite of the plate-sized steak ... Pippa proceeded to 'wrap herself around it'.

As she ate she watched Mrs. Cassidy with respect. The housekeeper was dealing with an almost incredible amount of meat.

'Because of our climate we have to cook as much as possible at once, Pippa,' she explained of the big roasts and rolls she was tucking into the vast oven, 'then pack as much as we can into the freezer, and salt all that's suitable for salting. Salt beef is for the boys when they're out with the herds. That, and damper, and black tea, is all they'll look at when they're overlanding. When they come in it's a different matter. They like a few fancy things then, even enjoy a slice of cake.' Mrs. Cassidy laughed and floured another large joint.

Pippa asked if she could help at least with the dishes, but was told that that was the kitchen girl's job, that Rosie might be hurt to see Young Missus doing what she should be doing.

'You'll soon find your niche,' Mrs. Cassidy assured her, 'this place is big enough to supply niches for all the world, I sometimes think. I often wonder why they made the Inside so big.' As Pippa wandered outside she called, 'Tea's in half an hour.'

Tea! After all that steak! Laughing, Pippa went down to look for Davy.

She found him playing with the piccaninnies in a shady hollow, and he at once remonstrated, 'You should wear a hat, Pippa, there's ultra-violent rays, didn't you know?'

'Violet, darling.' – Crag's tuition, she thought. – 'I'll wear one next time. But' ... giving him the opportunity that he obviously awaited ... 'the piccaninnies don't wear hats.'

'It's because of their skin which has more protective pigs.' Davy must have been conscious that he was not exactly right, for he said hurriedly, 'I've been in with the book-keeper. There's a lot to do in Falling Star for a book-keeper. He has to check all the bills, and you should see the kitchen bill, but the book-keeper says that's mainly because orders are always for three months.'

'Yes, I expect you get through a lot of food in three months.'

'But not candles,' disbelieved Davy. 'Me and the bookie—'

'The book-keeper and I.'

'Yes, us – well, we were surprised at a thousand candles.'

'A thousand candles?' Pippa was surprised herself. She said foolishly that they had their own electric plant here. Even if they hadn't they wouldn't need a thousand candles.

'A thousand candles,' Davy informed her, 'is eight-four dozen take away eight. Me and the bookie ... I mean the book-keeper and I, us, we added it up, and we were very surprised. As the bookie ... the book-keeper says you'd think Crag would have ordered eighty-four dozen, or so many pounds, not a thousand candles.'

'Yes,' Pippa said absently. She was thinking of that first time she had gone to Ku and how Crag had told her of his father's and mother's life together. He had said, she recalled, that it was a thousand candles.

'Crag wouldn't mean it seriously, Davy.'

'Well, he shouldn't order it. The bookie ... the book-keeper is a very busy man, so I'll ask Crag if he really wants—'

'*No*, Davy!' – Why was she going on like this? she thought helplessly; it was obviously a silly error in the order, and anyway to forbid a child was only to rouse a child's curiosity, and she did not want anything more said about candles. Fortunately, however, Davy had lost interest. He took her arm and carefully introduced her to all his playmates. There was Harold-Jimmy, Joey, Bobby, Trevor, Dougie, Paulie, Gary.

'No girls?'

'They're playing houses,' said Davy with the disgust expected from boys. – So children were the same the world over.

All the gang were in for lunch, as it was called, but it could have been dinner, for it ran to three large courses, soup, beef, of course, a big boiled pudding.

Pippa enjoyed the company of the stockmen again, with their 'distance' eyes, their rather old-world courtesy, their odour of ancient leather. The jackeroos, more her age, amused her with their competition in shirts and elastic-sided boots, their smart talk ... though she noticed that the last was kept to a minimum when Crag was around.

She had thought that Davy had forgotten the candles, but, a piece of potato poised aloft, he said, 'Crag, did you really mean a thousand candles on that grocery list to be brought out from town?'

'Davy!' remonstrated Pippa, and was annoyed at herself; it would have been better to have let the little boy have his say.

'Me and the bookie ... I mean the book-keeper and I ... we thought it was a lot of candles.'

'It is a lot, scrubber, but a thousand is the order.' As he spoke Crag was looking at Pippa, and she felt the pink mounting her cheeks.

Davy noticed the pink and reported, 'She never wore a hat. You'd better speak to your wife, Crag.'

'Reckon I will, scrubber, but at the proper time. Get

143

yourself around that spotted dog—'

'Spotted dog?'

'Now you're like Cass, she makes me say sultana pudding, but get yourself around it all the same, because after lunch you and Pippa are going out to watch a muster.'

'Oh, Crag!'

Pippa said nothing. She could scarcely refuse in front of all these men even if she wanted to, and she didn't want to, she wanted to be with Davy ... and she, too, wanted to see a muster.

They drove out in a different jeep, an extremely battered jeep, but evidently mechanically perfect, for it had no trouble with the bumps and rocks with which Crag confronted it. On a hill ... not really a hill, barely an incline, but now Pippa was seeing contours in the same way as the Insiders, Crag drew up the jeep for them to watch. The men and dogs were on the job, keeping the herd in a bunch, and Pippa noted the drovers sitting apparently relaxed in the saddle but actually sharp and alert.

'Mustering is funny,' said Crag by their side, 'sometimes I could drive you bang down the middle and nothing happen, another time it only needs the rattle of a stirrup. You never know when you're going to have a rush.' At Pippa's inquiring look he explained, 'A panic. A stampede.'

Even as he spoke, the mob began swinging. Pippa, who had been standing away from the jeep, turned sharply, and in doing so tripped and grazed her leg against the jeep wheel.

'It's nothing,' she said, embarrassed, as Crag immediately picked her up and put her into the back seat, lifting the injured leg to examine it. 'It's only a scratch.'

'Had your tetanus shots, Pippa?'

'Oh, for goodness' sake,' she laughed, 'it's barely touched.'

'But the jeep's old and rusty,' he fussed.

'Look,' she said, 'you only get tetanus in a deep wound. Don't be absurd, Crag.'

'All right,' he agreed, 'but at least we'll give you the earth treatment.'

She watched amazed as he made a poultice of water from the flask and some of the red earth not polluted by the wheels of jeeps or hooves of herds, then placed it on her leg.

'It's absolutely sterile,' he said, 'so not to worry.'

'It's an old aboriginal cure, Missus,' assured one of the stockmen, 'and I've seen wonderful results.'

'We don't recommend it, of course,' Crag went on, 'civilization has made it harder and harder to find the really sterile stuff. But if you're caught away from home, like we are, it's a good thing to remember.'

'Would it cure me?' asked Davy, standing and watching with interest.

There was silence. Then Crag bent over and made another poultice, a small one, and placed it carefully on Davy's small brow.

'Reckon so, scrubber,' he said. 'Well, folk, had enough?'

They saw camels on the way back, brumby ones whose ancestors had been brought in by the Afghans years ago. They were being herded by several cowboys ... Davy said it should be camelboys ... and seeing that the boy and Pippa were interested, Crag drove the jeep across the desert to where the camels were tethered.

The horsemen explained that a demand had opened up for camels, but that they had to be taught first to lead. Apart from the camel sales the men were hoping the station owners would pay them a premium for taking the camels away from their property, for it was well-known that they ate the precious scrub, knocked down fences and upset the waterholes.

Crag smoked his pipe as he listened, agreed as a station owner that they had a point there, but offered instead of a premium to buy a camel.

A broken-in, rather mild-looking fellow was brought forward, and Pippa was given the job of holding the tow rope as they led him back to Falling Star.

Here Davy had his first camel ride, and did quite well. Not so well Pippa, who did not care for the lunges forward, and when the animal dropped forward on its knees to let her off was so unprepared for the jolt that she somersaulted over its head. Davy adored that.

Crag taught Davy to say 'Hooshta' to get the camel started, then they left him adoring the camel, along with all the piccaninnies, and went inside.

'It's been a good day, Crag,' Pippa appreciated shyly.

'Tomorrow we'll go down to where I've enclosed the brumbies we caught last month. The stallions are due to be broken in, though most of the mares are finished.'

'You won't involve Davy in this?' said Pippa nervously.

'Oh, no,' he assured her, 'horse-breaking takes years of learning. Though I've no doubt that one day the scrubber—'

'Crag ... please!' She turned away.

'It could be true,' he said stubbornly. 'I mean you don't *know*, Pippa.'

'The doctors knew.'

'But they also admitted that miracles can happen. How do you know that today a miracle didn't happen?'

'That poultice of red earth? Oh, Crag!'

'I really meant how do you know that somewhere

146

someone didn't discover what we want discovered. But' … poking at his pipe … 'that red earth will do for a miracle right now, Pippa. You know what? The young 'un believes in it, he asked me was it all right to wash it off now that it had cured him. He has belief, and that's a cure in itself.'

She nodded, unable to reply.

The next day, as promised, Crag drove them down to the horse-break. The brumbies were enclosed in a well-grassed saucer of land by the lagoon, that is well-grassed by Inside standards. The lagoon at present was nicely filled, and insects were weaving flight patterns over it, frogs croaking a raucous chorus.

The jeep rimmed the shore until it reached the enclosure. Already the jackeroos and several of the stockmen were there, and one of the jacks was cutting out the ponies selected for the break, comprising a mare which had been put back from the former break because she was touchy and the first of the stallions.

The other jack started the break with the touchy mare, unsatisfactorily in the beginning, the same, the jack called to Crag, as last time, and then, on Crag's advice, using a more gentle approach, and soon achieving success.

'She only needed sympathy,' said Crag to Pippa. 'Mares most often are like that, we don't have much trouble with them.' He was eyeing a stallion thoughtfully. 'With good handling and good sense, stallions are no great worry, either, but I don't know about that fellow there. He's all of seven or eight years, I'd say, and wild stallions of that age get set in their ways.'

'He's pretty, Crag,' said Davy, and Pippa agreed with her brother. The stallion was a bright bay with a cream forehead and cream feet. But his eyes were unfriendly … even more than that, thought Pippa, they smouldered.

Crag approached him quietly, standing in front of him with a noose wide open, no pretext at all. Pippa had the idea that Crag felt as she did, that it would be no use trying to deceive this fellow. Crag dropped the loop over him, and beside her Pippa heard Davy draw in a deep breath.

The stallion did not protest. He even waited while Crag opened and shut the gate, and after that he walked quietly for several circles with Crag, then repeated his docile waiting when Crag returned him to the enclosure.

'You've done it, Crag, you've done it!' called Davy excitedly when Crag came back to their side. 'You've got him round. He likes you.'

Crag attended his pipe. He was thoughtful.

'Well, haven't you, Crag?' asked Davy impatiently.

'The trouble is, I don't know, scrubber, I don't know at all. I think I'll be watching that fellow. He's much too quiet for my liking. I feel he's looking me over. It isn't normal for a stallion like he is not to fight the rope.' Crag turned to Pippa and instructed in a low voice: 'You'll keep the scrubber away.'

'Of course.' She added in her turn: 'And you'll keep the piccaninnies off.'

'What made you say that?' They were walking back to the jeep now. 'What brought the little fry into it?'

'Cass was telling me how your mother and her mother took over that part of the station. I'd like to, too.' She paused. 'While I'm here.'

'You needn't have added that,' he reproached, 'you're here for ever.' At her quick look he reminded her, 'It doesn't matter how short a time is, it still is for ever. I think I told you that.'

'You told me for Davy.'

'Then it's for you, too.' He had started the jeep and

148

they were rimming the lagoon again towards home. 'What the heck . . .' he began.

She saw he was looking at a plane that must have come in during their absence, but, in the noise of hooves, had not been heard. It now sat in the middle of the row of upturned white plastic buckets that marked the run-in.

'Doug wasn't expected till next week,' he puzzled. 'Someone must have chartered him across.'

Pippa did not take much notice. She knew no one here, so felt it would be no concern of hers.

But as the jeep approached the homestead, a figure emerged from the house to stand on the wide verandah, and Pippa's heart lurched. She did know the passenger. It was her concern.

Rena waited there.

It was Crag who spoke first after they had alighted from the jeep and climbed the four shallow steps to where Rena stood and smiled brightly at them.

'Well,' he greeted drily, 'of all the people I wondered about Doug flying in, the last I thought of was you.' He kissed her cheek.

'Now, darling, none of that,' she laughed back, kissing him on the mouth, 'you've been expecting me for a year.'

'You took your time.'

'But the end is the same.'

'No, Rena, it's not. You see—'

'Pippa, how brown you are,' interrupted Rena. 'I hope you don't mind, I've put myself in your room. I've lots to tell you, so I thought we'd be girls together.'

'There are plenty of rooms,' came in Crag, 'if you'd let us know—'

'I didn't let you know because I wanted to surprise you.'

149

'You did.'

'A pleasant surprise? Darling, don't fuss. Two rooms are quite enough. Two boys. Two girls. What else? Talking of boys, where's my other laddie, my Davy? I must see him.' She turned round, evidently having seen Davy dart down to the piccaninnies, and she ran lightly towards him, calling his name. He turned and ran to her. Everyone would have to run to Rena today, never had she looked lovelier.

Pippa stood very still waiting for Crag to speak. When he didn't, she darted a quick look at him and was surprised at his thoughtful expression, thoughtful as his own eyes followed Rena.

'Crag . . .' Pippa breathed.

'Look here, Pippa—' But Crag was not to say it. One of the jacks came galloping up from the horse-break to tell the boss that a native stockman, Bobby, had been hoof-grazed by the bay stallion while he tried to put on a saddle and blindfold.

Rena at once was out of Crag's mind. 'The fool! I didn't want that done. I wanted him watched for a while. How badly hurt is Bobby? No, never mind, I'll ring A.A., anyway.' He turned on his heel and hurried in to pick up the telephone.

Pippa half attended to him and half attended to Rena. Her arm around Davy, she was coming up to the house.

'Air Ambulance?' she heard Crag call. 'I think I have a case for you. Crazy sort of stallion and a too-eager boy. Reckon he might need hospitalization . . . some shots, anyway, so if you're out this way . . . That soon? Good.' The telephone went down.

Now it was Pippa's turn to forget Rena. She watched fascinated as a precise routine took over. The tabletop truck was brought out and a mattress put on it, and the truck . . . with Crag . . . was driven down to the horse-break. Anticipating what would be needed next, Pippa went inside and gathered up blankets and pillows, and was waiting with them when Crag, sitting beside the prone patient at the back of the truck now, came up to the house.

He took a look at the blankets, and commended, 'Good girl, that's what I came for. Hop on, Pippa, and see how it's all done.'

'Is Bobby very bad?'

'He has a heck of a shock. That stallion was kidding them, pretending to play ball with them, then suddenly the boyo turned on the lightning. I think the bay could be a wrong 'un.'

'Do you have many?'

'No, and even when we do we can generally do something about it, but not when they're this feller's age. Here comes A.A. now. It's lucky we have plenty of space at Star, the A.A. is a bigger craft than the one the Flying Doc whizzes around in.'

By this time the plane was down, and two nurses climbing out, behind them two men, the pilot and the doctor. Pippa had a quick glimpse of resuscitators and oxygen apparatus before she was introduced to Doctor Todd, Nurse Brown, Sister Snell and the Captain.

'Mrs. Crag,' Crag said.

Bobby, the pain catching him quite severely now, was administered a shot, then the mattress was transferred to a light stretcher on wheels, a ramp put down and the patient edged in. There was the beat of engines again, the loud acceleration, then the few tree tops the station possessed moved in a sudden current of air, and the mercy flight was on its way.

'Will Bobby be all right?' asked Pippa.

'He'll be fine. A lot of his fineness, mark you, will be his importance. He would never have been up in a craft before. I try to take the boys up from time to time, but the trouble is there's not much time, and a lot of boys.'

'You have your own plane?'

'Surely,' he smiled.

For a while Pippa had forgotten Rena, but now, bumping back again, she remembered, and she knew she must speak with Crag. But somehow the words wouldn't come. She heard herself asking instead how the ambulance operated, heard him replying that all the Up Toppers paid a fee into it, and it was the best money they ever spent.

By now, the tabletop was nearing the house, but Rena did not meet them on the verandah this time, and when a bevy of men pounced on Crag to learn about Bobby, Pippa turned and went up the steps, down the hall to her room.

Their room. For another bed had been brought in. On it, surrounded by her clothes, sat Rena.

She looked up as Pippa came in, and spoke first.

'How is the stockman?' she asked, and took out, shook and hung up a blouse.

'He'll be all right.' Pippa knew that her cousin had not inquired out of concern but had merely used Bobby for the opener for whatever it was she had to say. For there were things to say. She had indicated that when she had laughed at Pippa on the verandah and told her: 'Girls together.'

'Tiresome of us,' continued Rena calmly, 'to have that episode staged just when we're itching to chatter.'

'It must be more tiresome for Bobby. It could have been disastrous. That stallion . . .' Pippa gave a little shiver.

'Nonsense.' Rena spoke airily. 'A horse can be managed if you go about it the right way. I'm sure I could go down now—'

'Rena, *don't!*' Pippa's voice was sharp. 'He's wild, he's

quite set in his ways. Crag said he could be a wrong one.'

'Yes, Crag.' Rena ran her tongue round her lips.

So it was to begin.

The older girl took out a frock now. She put it carefully on a hanger. She had a lot of clothes as though she intended to – stay.

'Well,' Rena demanded at length, 'aren't you wanting to hear about your dear cousin? For that's what I've come about, to get you up to date. That ... and something else.

'But first' ... briskly ... 'my present position. Well, Pippa, it's exactly as before.'

'I didn't expect it to be changed this quickly,' admitted Pippa. 'I mean legal things take time.'

'They take longer when they're not even begun. Yes, that's true. Mr. Callow hasn't filed any papers for me, and on my instruction will not do so.'

'You said this at the will-reading, but I thought you might have changed your mind, Rena. For you're entitled to everything, there would be no trouble, as your solicitor pointed out. I'm quite sure that when Uncle Preston made the new will he had your ultimate protest in mind.'

'Oh, yes, he would,' agreed Rena contemptuously, 'he would see me going cap in hand ... isn't that a ridiculous phrase these days? ... to Domrey Hardy. That certainly would be in Father's thoughts. Only it wasn't, and it isn't, and it never will be in mine. When I raced out from Uplands, Pippa, it was to give myself a thinking space, though I knew even then that I would never appeal. However, I made myself consider, and I reached the same decision. *And*' ... coming back from the wardrobe, where, typical of Rena, she had taken three-quarters of the space ... '*I came to another decision.*'

She waited for Pippa to ask it, but something cold had settled in Pippa, and she could not speak. She just sat there frozen, somehow knowing what Rena was going to say, wishing she could stop her.

When it became patent that she was not going to ask, Rena smiled slightly and began to speak.

'You heard poor Crag just now with his reproachful "You took your time." I did, I'm afraid. I've been a real trial to that darling man. For he's crazy about me, you know. Always has been. Always will. But' ... quietly now, watchfully ... 'he was also set on a family life, someone to bring up on Falling Star, someone to take over the station when he, like his father grew too old, grew old. And that's *why*, Pippa dear, he ... well ...' She gave a careless shrug. 'Oh, I'm not blaming you, darling,' she began again. 'I mean how could you tell how I felt? I've never been the emotional kind.'

'Felt? *You* felt?'

'Yes.'

'For – for—'

'For Crag.' Rena nodded. 'Yes, I loved Crag. I always have. It's always been Crag really, Pippa.'

'But, Rena, it hasn't ... it hasn't.' Pippa heard the shrill break in her voice but did not care. 'It hasn't. You know it hasn't.'

'Oh, darling, don't get carried away. You'll be quite all right. Crag's nothing if not generous – why, you'll have more than you would have ever had from Father or me.'

There was a pause ... for Pippa an incredulous pause ... then Rena calmly resumed.

'You must have seen Crag's face when I confronted him just now. You must have seen his eyes following me. It's always been like this, but I ... yes, I admit it ... I've treated him abominably. I played with Glen Burt. I—'

'Did you play with Domrey Hardy?' Pippa could not have said why she inserted that.

At once a change came over Rena. She went a grey-white. 'I never played with him. I – I loathe him.' She stopped talking for quite a while and went and stood by the window.

Minutes ticked by. Pippa thought: All this is a dream. It's too impossible. Surely Rena must know that Crag and I ... that we ... In a little village like Tombonda she must have heard—

Rena was coming back from the window.

'I'll never return to the Highlands,' she stated definitely.

'But *Crag* returns to Ku.'

Rena winced, then said, 'He'll dispose of Ku.'

'He loves it.'

Her cousin looked narrowly at her, then she said clearly, 'He loves me.'

'Rena ... Rena, this is going too far. There is something you must know. You can't know it or you wouldn't be talking like this.'

'Oh, yes.' Rena was lighting a cigarette now, exhaling idly. 'I did hear some fancy tales about you.'

'About *us*. About Crag as well as me. You see, we were – we were—'

She stopped incredulously as Rena went into peals of laughter. 'Darling, don't tell me that absurd rumour was true?'

'It was ... it was. If you want proof—'

'Want proof?' The laughter had left Rena. She was cold and hard as she often was. 'Haven't I proof here?' She looked around her.

'What do you mean, Rena?'

'This room.' Rena indicated the four walls, the space between the walls. 'This room, darling, *I* will be sharing with you. Girls together, remember? Do you think Crag of all people would stand for that? I know Crag very well. I've known him for years. He's never halfway. He's all man. Why, he wouldn't put up with his "wife" ' ... a small laugh ... 'next door to him any more than he would abide that stallion down there beating him.'

'Then you're wrong. He's come to a decision about the stallion. He says he's no good.' – Oh, why was she talking about irrelevant things like this? Pippa wondered blankly.

Rena was laughing softly, confidently. 'I'll soon change his mind about that, too, though, being Crag, I don't believe it will need any changing. However, it was the similarity I really meant, the no half-measures. For that's Crag. He goes the entire way.'

There was a pause, then:

'Darling, I did hear about that caper of yours, and I sympathize with you – after all, you had your brother to think of, and after all, Crag is something of a catch. But I'm afraid I didn't take it very seriously. I mean I did admit it could happen, and as you now tell me, and I do believe you, Pippa, you needn't produce any marriage lines, it has. But not' ... with an undertone now ... 'as I intend to take notice of. When I saw his room – and your room this afternoon, I'm afraid I *smiled,* Pippa. Crag would never accept that sort of wife. I think he went overboard for Davy, he always had a strong paternal streak, and I think because of that—

'But don't worry, Pippa. Everything will be all right, dear. I promise you I'll encourage Crag right to the hilt in any generosity he decides for you. But' ... thinly ... 'please don't give me that "marriage", because there never has been. *Has there?*' Rena waited a smiling moment, then went on.

'And now,' she said sweetly, 'away from intimacies.

Here's something you'll really want to hear. Before I came up I was in touch with Glen Burt. Oh, it was quite friendly. He's extremely nice once he isn't pursuing me.'

'Has he married Jennifer?'

Rena did not bother to reply to that. 'He said to tell you that a virus has been isolated in America, and that it's being worked on. That it could have reference to Davy.'

'Rena, stop. *Stop*!' Pippa got to her feet. She felt she was going mad. Not waiting for Rena's reaction, she ran to the door, turned the handle, closed the door behind her. Ran down the hall.

Once away from the house she raced blindly, unaware, uncaring where her feet took her. It was only when fatigue caught her up that she stopped, and fell, exhausted, to the ground.

CHAPTER EIGHT

SHE must have undergone a period of unconsciousness, or at least a blankness, for when Pippa opened her eyes the sun that had been well aloft was tottering on the edge of the horizon; even as she looked at it, it tipped right over, and where everything had been an antique gold, violet crept in, instead.

She was thankful that she had lain in a dwindling heat, for she had heard what the fierce rays of an Australian hinterland sun could do. But instead of feeling dehydrated, possibly alienated, all she was aware of was a great tiredness, natural enough after that foolish run. For it had been foolish, she realized that; she could have imperilled the lives of others who would have come out looking for her as well as destroy herself. She might even ... hearing the engine of a small plane, probably Crag's plane ... have imperilled someone now.

She got to her feet, ready to wave the moment she saw the craft overhead. But the plane did not come into sight, so it must have taken the opposite direction.

Biting her lips at the trouble she had caused, she looked around her. She had not anticipated any problem of direction, for although she had run blindly she considered she had not run all that long; the heat and her emotion would have seen to that. But although the terrain was flat as ever, she could see no distant buildings. She could not even glimpse the glitter of the lagoon. She forced herself to consider from which direction that beat of the plane engine had seemed to come, for that would be the field with the upturned white plastic buckets, and once she found it, she was near enough to home.

Home? She felt around that word sensitively, and knew with bitterness that she should have said homestead. If she were Mrs. Crag of Yantumara it should be home, but was she Mrs. Crag? Oh, yes, she had a marriage certificate, but was she Mrs. Crag? She remembered Rena's smiling face as she had said: 'Don't give me that "marriage", there never has been.' She had said '. . . not as you'd notice, and not as I intend to take notice of.' She had said: 'Crag would never accept that kind of wife.'

What kind of wife? What kind of marriage? Why hadn't she answered Rena when Rena had challenged tauntingly: 'Because there never has been. *Has there?*' Had it only been because of Davy that she had come wildly out here or had it been because she had nothing to answer to Rena? Only that night of which Crag had said:

'It's nothing. No ties tied. Relax.'

But had he not assured that, would she have remained there with Rena, would she have answered her: 'Yes, there has.' Would she have said that?

Pippa stood very still . . . and knew she would.

For she loved him. She was aware of it in that moment, aware that somewhere deep down in her she had known but not recognized it all along. She loved Crag, but to him it was 'no ties tied' . . . 'nothing' . . . 'relax'. Worse than that, Rena had come and now she stood between Crag and Rena, a pitiful little barrier, only there because a man had been drawn to a child.

Oh, Crag, she thought, what am I to do?

She had not realized she had called it aloud until a matter-of-fact small voice said, 'Crag's up in his plane with Ludy, Pippa, taking her into Minta Base Hospital to see Bobby. Bobby is Ludy's husband. Why did you come out here?'

It was Davy, hand-in-hand with a small brown boy he

introduced as Brucie.

'Brucie Indian-scouted after you,' Davy informed her next, 'only it wouldn't be Indian, would it? He's showed me how.'

'Oh, darling!' In her relief to get away from her torment, if only temporarily, Pippa hugged her brother, and for the first time she could remember he struggled free. At times he had wriggled uncomfortably, but mostly he had accepted caresses. Now he said quite gruffly, 'You don't do that, Pippa, not in front of name belonga Brucie.' He was picking up pidgin quickly.

'Sorry,' Pippa apologized, recognizing his new status. 'Well, I suppose we'd better start walking, it's getting quite dark.'

'Falling Star is only over there.' Davy waved nonchalantly. 'Just past the hill.' Pippa smiled ruefully. She had forgotten these infinitesimal inclines that could blot out all that lay beyond.

'Can I have tea with Brucie?' Davy was asking.

Pippa was not sure about that, not sure if the rations down the gully could include an extra, so she got round it by suggesting that Brucie had tea with them. 'I think Cassy will find room.'

'Plenty of room,' nodded Davy. 'The table will be empty. The stockmen are out, Crag's gone, and so has Rena.'

'Rena gone?'

'With Crag,' said Davy. 'Come on, Pippa, Brucie's hungry.' He waited, though, for Brucie to make the first indicative move, for in spite of his scouting tuition he was really as uncertain as Pippa which direction to take.

Brucie knew, though, and stepped out unfalteringly, whereupon Davy stepped out, too.

It was only Pippa who stumbled, and that was not because of any doubt of her direction, not with a scout like

Brucie. It was because of tears in her eyes.

So Rena had gone. With Crag.

She never would have found her way back without the scout. Pippa realized this as she trudged along behind Brucie and Davy, she acknowledged fully the mystery of this red terrain where, only half a mile from a point, that point was no longer visible or even familiar. She wondered how Brucie, even though it was his country, went so unfalteringly. Everything around her seemed exactly the same, so how could Brucie tell?

'The wind on the sand,' instructed Davy importantly when she said this, 'the way that tree bends.' The sand was all as red and all as rippled, and the tree was another mulga, and to Pippa it bent the same as all mulgas. She determined, unless by some miracle she achieved Brucie's scouting powers, never to run out like that again.

Back at the house she was relieved to find that her absence had not been noticed, or anyway, noted. Mrs. Cassidy must have thought she was in her room, or . . . a wince that Pippa despised herself for . . . even seeing the plane off. Quickly she proffered, 'I've been looking around Falling Star, Cassy.' Davy had not come in with her, so she was able to ask casually, 'Did I hear Crag's plane go out?'

Mrs. Cassidy looked up. 'Yes.' A pause. '*She* went with him.'

'Miss Franklin?'

'Yes.'

Another pause. Then: 'What's she here for, Pippa?'

'I . . . well, there was a message concerning Davy.'

'There are always letters,' said Mrs. Cassidy. 'There are phones.' She tossed her head.

'This was personal,' said Pippa. Well, Davy was personal, he was hers, because of him she was here at Yantumara, because of him she had married Crag. – Or that had been what she had thought.

Mrs. Cassidy did not pursue the subject of Rena, whom obviously she did not like. 'You look tired, dear. Did you walk too far?'

'No, not too far. The boys came after me. Davy wanted to have tea with Brucie tonight, but I thought if you didn't mind Brucie could have tea with us.'

'I don't mind, but probably Brucie will,' smiled Mrs. Cassidy. 'It's as Crag said, there's nothing like rib bones cooked over eucalyptus leaves.'

'Can I help you, seeing we have an extra?'

'You can supervise Rosie setting the table if you like, she has a habit of putting the knives and forks back to front.'

As Pippa corrected the knives and forks, she asked Cassy: 'Is Bobby any worse?'

'Oh, no, but Minta rang to say he would be better with someone by him. "Patients' relations" is a very big factor in hinterland hospitals. When I was growing up it was father, mother, sisters, brothers, uncles, aunts, then cousins, second cousins, right down the list. If you didn't allow them around the patient just pined to death. But it's getting different, and so long as Bobby has his wife he'll be all right.' With a sympathetic look at Pippa that made Pippa want to glance the other way, Mrs. Cassidy added, 'Miss Franklin would have been taken along just for Ludy, dear. Mostly the men are very thrilled to fly, but the women are a little apprehensive, and need a companion. If you'd been here I'm sure—'

'Yes,' said Pippa, but *she* was not sure. Not sure that if she had been there it would still not have been Rena accompanying Crag.

Brucie, as Cassy had said, was not over-impressed with the meat course, but certainly impressed with the ice-cream that Cassy gave the little boys instead of the adults' caramel rice.

After the dishes had been put in the dishwater, Pippa went and sat on the big verandah with the book-keeper and those of the stockmen and jackeroos not out with the herds. It was a velvet night, as velvet as only hinterland nights could be, she decided, an exaggerated gold moon, stars so big you felt you could pluck them down. It was not the sort of night to sit alone . . . yes, alone, even with seven men. It was a night for one man.

She wanted to ask how long Crag would be away, but the words would not come. She waited until it was time to call Davy to bed, then after she had bathed him, heard his prayers, something that Crag had taken over from her, she, too, went to bed. Rena's things were strewn all around the room. It didn't seem Pippa's own room any more. But then it wasn't, it was their room. Girls together, Rena had smilingly said.

With a little sigh she tidied up some of the things that had tumbled from Rena's bags, scarves, blouses, the beautiful negligées she had always had . . . and a photo in a leather case. Only a small photo. Able to be fitted . . . as it was . . . in the fold of a handkerchief. Pippa looked down on it and smiled as she saw the rather crafty yet likeable face of naughty old Uncle Preston, Rena's father. Then her glance fell on the other side of the case. Dom. Domrey Hardy. What was the overseer, whom Rena despised so heartily, doing there?

She closed the folder, freed the bed in case Rena did come in late, though she knew that an aircraft could never put down here at night without a flare, then clicked out the light.

She did not go to sleep for a long time. Although she knew that Rena . . . and Crag could not come, she could not help herself from listening for them. But at last in the small hours, sleep took over, and she was still asleep when Rosie brought in her tea.

Her first glance went to the bed, but it was still unoccupied. Well, she had known that.

Then Rosie said, 'You look for Miss, Missus, she not home all night. Boss, too.'

'I expect that.' Pippa accepted the tea.

'Yes, but those two,' went on Rosie, 'they come back all right, but not here.' She gave some actions. 'They have trouble with no gas for that plane, so they put it down in Western Field and stay in the stockies' hut.'

'How – how do you know this?' Pippa held tightly to her tea.

'Our Billy, him going past that hut when Boss tells him to get someone to bring gas for plane to get back. Bobby's all right, Billy says, and Ludy is stopping with him. You bin like more tea?'

'No, thank you, Rosie, I'll get up.'

When she went down to the kitchen, Cassy repeated Rosie's story.

'Evidently Crag wanted to get home yesterday and left as soon as he had deposited Ludy with Bobby at the hospital. But he mustn't have checked as he always checks, either that or the engine was amiss, for they had to come down at Western Field while it was still light. Billy was going past rounding up some stragglers, and Crag instructed him to get fuel out today. Why don't you go along, dear?'

'No. Nó, I don't think so. I – I thought I would have a morning with the mothers and the piccaninnies.' She hadn't thought so, not for this morning, anyway, though she had intended to do it one day, and she knew she could not bring herself to go out there.

She heard the jeep put off later with its succour but did not look up. – Also she did not let herself think of last night. She thought of another night outside a tent, a navy blue night with a sliver of moon. Somewhere a pheasant, somewhere a wood pigeon. Soft earth and a tree leaning over. It all seemed unreal now. Perhaps it had never been.

Then she thought of Rena, Rena so lovely that any man's head would be turned, and especially a man who had loved her once. And loved her still? 'If you're coming, Pippa,' Davy reminded reproachfully by her side.

'I'm coming, darling.'

Down in the gully, no actual gully, really, just a slight indentation and probably indented like that by many feet passing over it for many years, for Cassy had told Pippa that for as long as she could recall meetings had been held there, it had been a discussion place, the gins were shy at first, but still friendly. The piccaninnies, however, having heard all about her from Davy, flocked around at once, and their mothers, following up to scold them, remained instead, and soon all the women were talking together.

Children predominated the conversation, of course, didn't children always? ... and Pippa heard how Mary's Elizabeth was three and the eldest four and how last year Janey's Gary had got ruddy fever ... scarlatina, Pippa decided ... and passed it around the camp. Janey was very proud of that achievement.

The pics got tired of the conversation and wandered off, but their mothers remained to talk eagerly with Pippa. Like all women, they were keen on dressing up, even though it was true that right now they wore very little. 'But,' they giggled, 'when that hairy feller comes we buy very good cloes, Missus, you'll see when Mr Walker calls.'

One of the jackeroos had joined the group to call Pippa up for tea, and he explained, 'We call the Afghan hawker . . . yes, he has long hair and a beard, hence he's the hairy feller . . . Mr. Walker because his own name is quite a mouthful. There's not many of these unique characters left now. Once they were the only Up Top itinerant salesmen. I doubt if you'll find anything maddeningly exciting in Mr. Walker's bags, but the gins adore his beads, scarves and baubles.'

After morning tea, Pippa returned to the gully again, and on an invitation from the women went into their houses. She decided that as far as health went, they were very well catered for. The homestead kept a close eye on their general condition and a specially close eye on any possibility of leprosy, once a danger out here. Also, a Government glaucoma team called every year.

But education, she thought, was sadly lacking. Over lunch later the men who had been left behind for their rest periods said that Crag was trying to contend with this by correspondence, only it was difficult to find someone to superintend the lessons. One of the stockmen asked Pippa if she had written yet for Davy's enrolment. 'It's a good system,' he said, adding modestly that it was the only instruction he had had, whereupon the others at the table laughed uproariously and advised Pippa to have nothing to do with it.

'Seriously, though,' they added when the laughter had died down, 'Snow's right, it does teach the kids, and you need have no fear that the young 'un is missing anything by not going to school.'

Davy had never been to school, either she or Aunt Helen had taught him everything he knew, so Pippa knew it would be no miss. But a sudden thought came to her that here could be the niche she needed. She could superintend the lessons, Davy's and the pics'. Perhaps Crag could even allot a little schoolhouse from the many buildings. She would be like his mother and his grandmother, she thought, she would be a true countrywoman. She felt enthusiasm bubbling through her ... then hollowly came the realization that it would be no good. What was the use of thinking of schoolrooms when before anything could eventuate she would be gone? What was the use of thinking about lessons for Davy when—

She did not go back to the gully that afternoon.

The day wore on. She would have thought that Crag and Rena would have been in by now, but the jackeroo informed her that it was a fair run out by jeep so they could not be expected until late afternoon. When late afternoon grew into night she found herself listening so hard that her ears throbbed. She did not want her evening meal, but she forced it down, hoping that Cassy and the men did not notice her preoccupation.

'Cessna must be playing up, so Crag's coming in by the jeep,' decided Snowy. 'But don't you fret, Mrs. C., you'll have your man back tonight.'

She tried to smile back at Snowy's kindly face, but it was a hard try. Mrs. C. That was Crag's tag for her. But *your man*. That was not, and never had been, and never could be, a tag for him.

She did the usual after-dinner things, she sat for a while on the verandah with the others, then she called Davy from the gully, bathed and bedded him. What a much more independent little boy he was becoming, she thought. He took over most of the washing himself, and told her after she had tucked him in that she needn't leave on a light. He even did not ask as much about his idol Crag. So a little boy was growing up.

But ... achingly ... a little boy couldn't. He had only now one Australian spring.

She went to bed herself and could not have said at what time she heard the jeep coming in. It was Rena and Crag at last, she knew it by their voices that carried distinctly through the quiet night. They were on the verandah, and she heard Crag say: 'Impulse, Rena, impulse, that's all it was. How else can I drive it home to you ... how can I make you see it that way .. see how it's bringing chaos to the heart?'

'But, Crag ...' She did not hear Rena's answer and she did not want to.

So already Davy was an impulse to be regretted ... or was it what Crag had done because of Davy that was the regret? The chaos to a heart?

It was much later that Rena came in. Even in her numbness, Pippa was aware of the length of time that had passed. ...

When Pippa went along for breakfast the next morning, Rena, already the mistress, it seemed, having ordered Rosie to bring her breakfast to her bed, it was to learn that Crag had left very early. He had taken Davy and Brucie with him. They had gone, Cassy reported, to run down some scrubber steers that Crag had seen coming back from Western Field.

Pippa did not notice that she waved aside her usual concern for Davy, especially when his activities included running down scrubbers ... what had he reported to her? you do it in full gallop, leap from the horse, flick it by its tail and pin it to the ground ... to ask instead if there had been anything amiss with the plane.

'Yes, so they left it there and came back in the jeep. Mind you, though' ... a smile ... 'it was out of gas as well. If you ask me, Pippa, your man was so anxious to get home to you he forgot his usual check.'

Yes ... but he did not forget to linger on a verandah and say: 'Impulse, Rena ... you must see it that way ... see how it's bringing chaos to the heart.'

But it was no use going over things like this. So long as

she remained here she must occupy herself. Either that, or she could bear it no longer, and she had to, for Davy. So as soon as the meal was finished she went down to the book-keeper's office and asked Rupey for as much unwanted paper as he could spare. He found her a generous armful, then, when he learned that she intended starting off those of the pics who would sit still long enough on some elementary lessons, found pencils, too.

'There's manuals here,' he smiled, 'probably left over from Crag's young days, so not the latest methods, but at least they'd give you a pointer.'

Pippa thanked him and went off, calling back to him when he advised her not to be disappointed at her first attempt an assurance that she would not.

She had expected, with the book-keeper, that the pics would be bored with any attempt she made, that they would scribble over the paper, but to her delight they listened intently when she started them off, their pansy eyes big and grave, their little pencil marks on the paper thin and delicate.

It was there that Crag, having finished rounding up the scrubber steers and come home again, found her, and for a while he stood looking down on her.

'The hillside's dew-pearled,' he said softly.

'There's no hillsides here,' said Davy practically, 'unless you mean what we call the hills but are really only inclines.' He added indignantly as Crag smiled, 'You told me so yourself.'

'I was just wondering where a poet had gone,' said Crag, thinking of a little boy on a train who had told him that Pippa had been called that because she had been born at seven and had hillside eyes. 'You're a different scrubber now, Davy.'

'Of course I am, because I'm better. Ever since you poulticed me I've been cured. You said it made you better, and it did.'

'Then you're better,' agreed Crag.

He went over to Davy's sister. 'Well, Teacher?' he smiled.

'It is well,' she answered with shining enthusiasm in the green eyes he had been watching. 'These children are wonderful. If they can do that just sitting around me on the ground, imagine what they'd do in a proper feller school.'

Crag burst into laughter, Pippa, after some surprise at herself and the pidgin that, as with Davy, had crept in, laughing with him, then the pics and Davy at the madness of old people.

Rena joined them to ask about the mirth, and the mothers, never far behind their children, looked admiringly at the beautiful new miss with the lovely clothes.

'I'm afraid you've spoiled them for Mr. Walker,' smiled Pippa to her cousin as they went up the hill again, but Rena's smile back as Pippa explained about the Afghan hawker did not reach her eyes.

The old restlessness was on her. Pippa recognized it at once. How often had she seen that look on Rena at Uplands? That strange unrest. That unhappiness. Why was Rena unsettled like this?

For a moment she wondered longingly if her cousin's preoccupation was because of something that Crag had said to her . . . But no, not with an answer such as he had given her last night. Again she heard that: 'Impulse . . . you must see it . . . see how it's bringing chaos to the heart.'

'Crag.' Rena's cool voice cut into Pippa's pain. 'Crag, when are you taking me down to the horse-break?'

'Now, if you like.' He stopped to light his pipe.

'In a *frock*?'

'What did you expect to wear?'

'Jodhpurs at least,' she flung.

He took the pipe out of his mouth and looked seriously at her. 'What for, Rena? There'll be no riding down there.'

'Oh, Crag, don't be an old fuddy, I know as much about horses as you.'

'Southern Highland horses,' he agreed, 'but these are vastly different, Rena.'

'Oh, I know they've run wild,' she said impatiently, 'but I've handled horses that have been in the field all the year.'

'These have been in the scrub, Rena, all their lives. Most of them have never seen a man, never felt a rein.'

'I can look after myself.' She tossed her head.

'Perhaps, but you're not doing it down there.'

'We'll see about that.'

Quite obviously she was irritated, on edge. Pippa sensed, though she did not comprehend, Rena's urgent need to expend herself ... to escape from something that was enclosing her. Puzzled, Pippa glanced up to see how Crag was reacting.

He was reacting calmly ... but intentionally. 'Yes, we will see,' he nodded firmly. After a moment he offered equably, 'I'll get a pony up for you this afternoon.'

'Not a pony, Crag.' Rena's voice was shrill. 'What do you think I am, a week-end rider? I want a horse. I want that stallion I've been hearing about.'

'*No one* is going to try him any more. You know now, from going into Minta, what happened to Bobby.'

'Bobby's hands might not have been right. I have excellent hands for a strong-willed horse. Dom ... I mean I've often been told so.'

'I imagine you have been, Rena, but this is not just a strong-willed horse, this is a wrong 'un. What I should do

171

in these circumstances is very obvious, but what I'm going to do, being a fool I suppose, is take that feller right back to where he belongs.'

'To the scrub?'

'Yes.'

'But that's a terrible waste of a horse like that. He's a handsome thing.'

Sharply Crag said, 'Have you seen him, then?'

'Oh, yes, I had a quick look after breakfast.' She smiled at him, but Crag did not smile back.

'I'm not pleased with you, Rena,' he stated. 'The horse is unpredictable.'

'But then,' she came in, 'so are most things.'

'Rena, I'm not joking.'

'Neither am I.'

'You're not to go down to the horse-break unless I say and unless I'm with you.' He waited. 'Understand?'

'Very well.' She capitulated so completely and so unexpectedly that Pippa looked at her in surprise.

'Very well, darling,' she said again, and she leaned up and touched his cheek.

Uncomfortable at the closeness that Rena deliberately had established between herself and Crag, both physically as she stood in front of him and in the endearment she used, Pippa murmured an excuse and hurried ahead.

Through the bathroom window she could see Rena and Crag walking up together, Rena now being demure and submissive as she kept close to Crag's side. What is she doing, Pippa thought wretchedly, and why is she doing it? I still don't believe she really loves, or has ever loved, Crag, so why is she going on like this? – But she didn't ask herself how *Crag* felt, for she already knew; she had heard. She had heard – '. . . impulse . . . see it this way . . . chaos to the heart.'

The meal was an ordeal. Trying to appear normal. Trying to join the conversation. Trying even to eat. That last was very important, for several times Crag's keen eyes estimated her inroads on her laden plate, and he looked stern. Just how did he consider her, she wondered bleakly, simply as another child to be told what to do?

She heard the men at the table ... there was a full complement for the meal, for there was to be a strenuous afternoon programme and they were stoking up ... discussing the stallion again. Snowy had had an experience once like this and he suggested gelding the wild one, if it could be achieved, because often it availed a character change, and that feller certainly needed one, but Crag said no, the horse would go free, he was to be left alone, not touched. He was taboo.

He nodded this gravely to Rena, and she nodded docilely back.

And perhaps ... Pippa was to think this later ... her cousin really meant that agreement, perhaps if what subsequently happened that afternoon had not happened, Rena would have rested on her laurels, for laurels they must be, thought Pippa bitterly, hearing once more those words of Crag's to Rena last night.

But, the meal over and the men gone, and following Rena to hear more fully from her Glen Burt's report on Davy, the report she had interrupted before because she had been unable to listen any longer, the station telephone suddenly pealed, and Mrs. Cassidy came into the hall and picked it up.

From the moment it rang there was something electric in the air. Pippa could not have put a finger on it ... only a finger on Rena, who suddenly stood very still and looked white and strained. Her cousin could not possibly know, as she herself could not know, the identity of the caller, but she stood there *and she knew*. Pippa could tell she knew.

Cassy listened for a while, then said, 'Yes, I'll write that down.' Then she put the phone back.

'Rena, I want to discuss Davy and what Glen Burt told you,' Pippa began.

'Why didn't she read the message out?' Rena said stonily.

'It wasn't for us. It would be for Crag. Rena—'

'Why did she have to be so secretive?'

'She wasn't being secretive, it just wasn't our business. Rena—'

But Rena turned impatiently on her. 'I told you what he said,' she cried irritably. 'Now I'm going down to that horse.'

'Crag told you not to.'

'I know. Pippa, I *know*. But I have to do something. Can't you see that?'

'No.' Pippa looked back at her. Then she cried, 'Rena ... Rena!'

For Rena was running out of the room and down the steps.

She still had on her frock, so at least she would not try anything foolish, but, remembering Crag's injunction not even to be near the horse, Pippa went after her.

Halfway there, she turned back cautiously to check up on Davy, for she knew that Crag would want him ... as she did, too ... well away from the break. But she glimpsed her brother through the office window sitting at the desk with Rupie, probably checking the station accounts again, another job he had quaintly taken upon himself. She also saw that the piccaninnies were playing safely in the gully, so all, away from the break, was well.

When she got down to the enclosure, it seemed at first that it was deserted, then she noted that the recently broken mares and stallions were cropping quietly in one corral, the ones yet to be dealt with in another pen. But there was no sign of the bay stallion. She would have turned away, thinking that Rena had come and then gone in the belief that Crag already had done what he had said he would do, release the wrong one.

Then she heard the small noise from the barn that adjoined the inner enclosure. She went towards it, keeping well outside the fence, climbed the few rungs and peered in. It was dark after the sunlight, and for a while Pippa could not focus. Then she outlined the shape of two stalls. In one of them, crouched as far as she could from the intervening half-way wall, was Rena, and she was staring with fear ... Rena afraid! ... at the horse on the other side. It was the wild one. Evidently the men had got a rope over him and manoeuvred him inside.

He seemed quiet enough, but he was looking back at Rena, and even from where she watched Pippa could see the fiery red in his eyes, the red in his flaring nostrils. She could see that Rena could not move.

'I'll get help,' she said softly but clearly. Rena dared not answer back.

Pippa climbed quietly down and ran swiftly up to the homestead. As she raced she remembered sickeningly that Crag and all the men had gone out.

She was standing on the lower step of the verandah, wondering whether to summon Rupie, wondering what she could do, when she saw the private mail and hire waggon bumping along the station flat. It was not mail day, but never had the mail-man ... and the man sitting beside him ... been more welcome. Pippa was unaware that she was crying with relief.

Mrs. Cassidy had come out by now to greet the visitor, and she said, not noticing Pippa's anxiety, 'That was fast, if you like. A message to say you're coming and you're here!'

'The F.D. was going out to Crossroads, so I took my passenger that far. I brought him the rest.' The driver pocketed the fee the passenger handed him and said, 'Thanks, Mr. Hardy.'

Hardy. Domrey Hardy. Dom. For a moment Pippa heard again the phone call that had electrified Rena, she saw Rena's strained face. It had been Dom . . . *and Rena had known*. She had sensed, in the way people do sense when they are close, that— But Rena and Dom— *close*?

It didn't matter now, though, only a girl in danger mattered. She was running to the overseer, shouting his name, shouting incoherent things, yet they must not have been entirely incoherent, for Domrey Hardy began running with her. Running down to the break.

When they reached it, he pushed Pippa back firmly, then he mounted the fence. He peered in.

'Rena,' he said at last very quietly, 'it's me. It's Dom.'

Rena did not reply.

'The horse is no good,' he said next. 'The moment you turn it's going to knock down that wall, then strike. You know that, don't you? The only thing is for me to divert it as you scramble out. Do you follow me?'

It was several minutes before Rena spoke, then she said without any sign of the panic she must be undergoing, 'Since when have you told me about horses, Hardy?'

'Rena, don't be a damn fool.'

'I've ridden worse ones than these,' came the reply.

'Well, you're not riding this one now. Do as I say. When I divert the stallion, you—'

'I won't.'

'Then you won't come out alive.'

'Would that worry you?' Her voice came clear and contemptuous.

'It would be two deaths, and you must know it. Without you I ... Rena, I'm moving in now. Are you ready?'

'I'm stopping here.'

'Then the only thing for me to do is handle the horse myself.'

'You think you're capable?' Rena jeered.

'Oh, Dom, don't listen,' Pippa said urgently, for she had seen the man stiffen. She put out her hand to stop him, but he brushed it, though without anger, aside.

He said bitterly, seeing the danger, 'If it has to be this way ...' and he moved over the fence towards the stallion's stall.

What happened then happened so fast and so terrifyingly that Pippa felt it was like the frenzied flicking of a movie camera suddenly gone crazy.

Hardly had Dom moved forward than the stallion came at him like a hurricane, teeth bared, ears flattened, hooves raised high. As Rena screamed, Dom fell down and rolled over, rolled just in front of where the hooves struck, rolled again and again only a fraction of an inch from each cruel strike.

Now he was on his feet and jumping for the snubbing post, but it was clear that the stallion would get him before that.

Pippa stood sick and useless, seeing it all in those unrelated flicks again ... and then she heard the welcome swing of a rope, the scared mares in the next enclosure whinnying and galloping wildly round the fence, then the rope descending and pulling the stallion up.

It would not hold him for long, though ... the haltering rope had not succeeded in doing that ... so Crag, for it was Crag, wasted no time. He yelled for Pippa to stand clear, then he opened the gate and let the stallion out. One moment the horse was there, the next it was gone. Pippa did not watch where, she had turned to Dom

Hardy and Rena.

Dom was lying unconscious on the floor of the stall, and Rena . . . Rena was kneeling by his side . . . lifting his head on to her lap. She was crying, 'Dom! Dom! Oh, darling!'

The tears were streaming down her cheeks.

CHAPTER NINE

THE Flying Doctor had come and gone. He had examined Dom and reported no need for Air Ambulance to take him into Minta Base, not even a need to bring out a nurse. There was no concussion, no breaks or strains. By some miracle, or by some remarkable adroitness, Dom had missed those savagely flailing hooves. All he was suffering was a reaction from the horrifying minutes that had nearly cost him his life.

After they had taken Dom up to the homestead on an improvised stretcher, Rena by his side and holding his hand, then eased him into a bed, Pippa and Crag had stood on the other side of the bed to Rena, and in silence the three had waited . . . had watched the grey face.

But slowly the colour had begun to creep back, and by the time the F.D. flew in, Dom was breathing normally again. Yet when his eyes had looked up, Pippa had known that it was only Rena whom he saw, and when the F.D. said it was safe for the patient to be left so long as someone remained at hand to attend him if needed, there was no question who the attendant must be.

Pippa went out behind the two men and watched them as Crag nodded the doctor into the jeep then got behind the wheel. As the pair drove across the strip to where the doctor's Auster waited, she thought again of that anxiety in Rena's voice when she had knelt beside Dom . . . then Rena coming up from the break by Dom's side, Dom's hand tenderly in hers. Later, Dom's eyes as consciousness had returned, those eager eyes only aware of Rena.

What had happened once between those two? What would happen now? Most of all, when it did, what of

Crag?

She stood on the verandah a long time just staring into distance. Where was the wrong one now? she wondered. She hoped the stallion had regained his old haunts, for somehow she could feel no anger against him, and she was glad that Crag had set him free.

Mrs. Cassidy came out with tea, and must have been thinking of the horse, too, for she said, 'Let's hope he doesn't pass his meanness on to any of next year's foals, or if he does that they're not caught in the round-up. Those sort are always dangerous.'

'Next year's foals?'

'It's spring,' reminded Mrs. Cassidy, 'and in spring . . .' She smiled at Pippa. When they had finished she took up the emptied cups and went back to the kitchen. But Pippa stopped on the verandah.

Spring. It couldn't be. It mustn't be! She looked around her in alarm, searching for it. There was nothing to proclaim it, not like it had been proclaimed in the springs she had known in England. She remembered Aunt Helen's garden . . . snowdrops, narcissi, blunt buds on trees burgeoning into miracles of petals, honey bees laden with sweet largesse. *That* was spring, not this barrenness, and yet, she recalled indignantly from Crag: 'It's the most spring in all the world.'

How could he have cheated them like this, even for the love of a small boy for whom he had taken a fancy? A small boy, she thought dully, who was now only an 'impulse', an impulse that, on Rena's arrival, had brought 'chaos to the heart'.

No, there was no spring here.

Yet . . . 'September is the first of spring,' Davy had sung, and if Cass was right about the season, then this was that spring she had left England for. It was Davy's final spring. She had borrowed Australian spring for him, but she could never borrow again, there would be no second chance. Ten months, Doctor Harries had said. So this – this nothingness was all that Davy would have.

She could not see the scene before her for angry tears, but one thing she must see, and that was a calendar. Running down the steps, she crossed to the book-keeper's office. There at least she should find the date.

Once more Davy was helping Rupie to check the accounts; he took these self-appointed jobs very seriously. He did not look up as she came in. She crossed to a wall almanac, where it was another self-appointed job of her small brother's to cancel each spent day. As she stood there she heard the Auster leaving, and knew that Crag would be waiting out there in the field, his wide hat tilted over his eyes against the glare, watching for the F.D. to hide himself in that vast inverted blue bowl. She came back to the calendar and saw that the last cancelling was August the thirty-first. If she had harboured any disbelief the piles of accounts on the desk would have been witness to the end of the month. So it *was* the first of spring.

She turned desperately away, but Rupie called, 'Did you want anything, Mrs. Crag?'

What would he say, she thought dully, if I answered that I want time, I must have more time for Davy, can you bring some time out of your stock cupboard, Rupie, the way you brought out Crag's old school manuals?

'I see you haven't cancelled Crag's thousand candles,' tut-tutted Davy busily, checking a long list, still unaware of his sister. 'Did you speak to him about his mistake?'

'Yes, but he said it wasn't a mistake. He said he wanted a thousand candles and there seemed no other way.' Rupie scratched his head in bewilderment, whereupon Davy did the same.

'Perhaps it's for a party,' suggested Davy.

'Some party!'

'Some party,' copied Davy. 'Now, what about all this rice?' He looked disapprovingly at the list, no doubt seeing many rice puddings, which he disliked. Instinctive laughter bubbled up in Pippa . . . but at once it died down again. Time, she was thinking painfully, is running out. She turned away.

She did not know she was running herself until she ran into Crag. He had come back from the field, but the jeep was still on the drive, and when they collided, he wheeled her swiftly to the waggon, and the next moment they were bumping down to the gate.

'Crag,' she said bitterly, 'why did you tell me – tell us—'

'Sorry, Pippa, let me be first. Because I have to show you something. It must have happened yesterday.' He was drawing up the jeep now, sweeping her out and down to one of their few little gullies. She had never noticed this small scoop before, and she cried out in pleasure at its tiny saucer of water, and there in the middle of the water actually one pink lily, now past its prime, almost drooped down . . . but it had bloomed.

'Spring,' said Crag proudly, 'was yesterday. Now what did you want to say, Pippa? Pippa. Pippa – Oh, my little love . . .'

For Pippa was crying, crying brokenly. It seemed bitterly unfair to her that this was the last offering for Davy. 'You told me . . . you told us . . .' Then abruptly her words were trailing off in a wonder instead of a resentment. *Had* Crag just said: 'My little love'?

She looked up at him, looked extractingly. So he, too, had caught that glance between Dom and Rena, and now that he was out of the running, out of a lovely girl's heart, he was trying for a second-best.

'Don't cry, tell me, Pippa,' Crag was urging.

'This isn't spring,' she answered, coming back to Davy, 'only one withered flower. So Davy has had his last spring after all.' She looked at him with accusation as though he had done it himself.

'I'm sorry that it's all we have to offer,' he admitted humbly.

'But you said it was the most spring in all the world.'

'It was once . . . five years ago,' he recalled. 'There were carpets of flowers, forests of grass. This place occasionally does miracles like that. Who knows, Pippa, there may be another bursting another year.'

'You said there was the most spring—' she repeated doggedly.

'I also said "sometimes",' he sighed. As she still looked at him in anger, he went on, 'If it's not next year we'll have to wait for the year after . . . then the year after that But while we're waiting . . . the *three* of us, Pippa . . . the doctors will be finding something for Davy. Rena has told me what Glen Burt said . . . what could come from this new breakthrough.'

'But it has to be now, not then, otherwise—'

'Don't you believe that. I put a poultice on him, remember?'

'Oh, don't be foolish, Crag.'

'Don't *you* be, Pippa. The scrubber believed in that poultice, and I do, too. I really mean I believe in his belief, so we'll keep him believing, and we'll keep him waiting for spring. And we'll keep this' . . . he plucked out the lily . . . 'just between us.'

'But it takes more than that,' she said dully, 'it takes more than belief and a poultice.'

'Then I have it for you. The F.D. has been looking Davy over regularly . . . you didn't know that, did you? The last time he did he said: "This boy is coming back to us so fast I can't keep up." '

183

'Oh, Crag, he didn't say that. Doctors don't.'

'All right then, he said "Pulse ... temperature ... breathing ... metabolism." He said the rest. After which he said "I'm amazed." Yes, Pippa, that's true.'

She stood dumbly, knowing she mustn't believe it, though yearning to. Then she whispered, 'Crag, it can't last.'

'It has to last till spring. *One* spring. And I reckon Falling Star can keep on putting that back until the scrubber's good and ready. Look what we've done this time.' He threw the tired lily away.

She watched it flutter to the scoop of water, float there. 'Did the F.D. really say—'

'What a disbeliever you are! Do you want to ring him for yourself? You shouldn't need to, Pippa, you have your own two eyes.'

Yes, she had her eyes, and they had seen Davy's eyes, brighter and bluer than they had ever been. She had seen his little body, browner, firmer, stronger. She had seen ...

But could – *could* Davy wait?

Crag's arms were around her ... she had not noticed them slip there ... and he whispered, reading her as he always did: 'He'll wait, wife.'

She stiffened in the arms at that, remembering the 'second-best', and she said bleakly, 'I have to talk to you about that.'

'I have to talk to you about it myself, Mrs. Crag. Do you remember when we first started this fool arrangement—' Fool arrangement. So he was going to ask for a release.

'Yes,' she said.

'Do you remember the terms we made and how they could be broken?'

'Yes,' she said again.

'I made no firm promise . . . I left that much open . . . but I also said that until you said. . .' He looked at her and waited, but she did not speak.

After he had waited for a long while and she still did not speak he sighed, 'Just as well I left that loophole, Pippa, because I'm not wasting any more time. You're Mrs. Crag, and that's the way it's to be. Do you hear?'

'I hear, but I can't believe you. Not with "impulse" . . . "see it this way" . . . "chaos to the heart." ' As he looked back uncomprehending, she called angrily, 'Oh, Crag, can't you understand, I *heard*. I heard you and Rena talking on the verandah that night. – Crag?'

For Crag was laughing at her, saying, 'Oh, *that*!'

'That,' he went on, 'was for Rena. That was what impulse, Rena's impulse and Dom's impulse, had done to two people. It had brought chaos to the heart.'

'Then it wasn't *your* impulse of loving Davy?'

'Loving the scrubber was never that.'

'It wasn't *your* impulse of accepting me as well?'

'Pippa, in one minute I'll—'

'But I have to know, Crag. I have to know about Rena. You love her.'

'No,' Crag said.

'Then you loved her?'

'No,' he said again.

'You asked her to marry you.'

'In a way. It was after my father died . . . I was returning to Falling Star, and I thought how I would like a son, too . . . But you know all that. Perhaps I might never have come to it, asking her, I mean, had Rena not asked first. That's rotten of me, I know, but it's the truth. You must have seen yourself how it was afterwards with Glen Burt.'

She had seen it, so she could not deny it. She asked

helplessly: 'Why, Crag, *why* was she like that?'

'Because she was running away. Because pride, which was more predominant in Rena than I've ever seen it in anyone, stood in her way.'

'Running?'

'From Dom. She loved Dom. She loved him from the first moment she saw him ... over in England, I think it was. Because she was Rena and spoiled rotten ... yes, she was spoiled rotten, Pippa ... she had to "buy" him at once, or at least have her father "buy" him for her. Old Franklin was willing enough. He liked Dom.' Crag took out his pipe. 'Who wouldn't?'

Pippa murmured, 'Go on.'

'So they purchased the Highlands estate and made Dom the overseer.' Crag tapped the tobacco. 'With an end in view. But Hardy was as proud as Rena was. He loved her as much as she loved him, but he could accept no charity, and he wouldn't be bought. So—'

'So, Crag?'

'A man's stubborn pride stopped him asking what she waited for him to ask, and when Rena asked instead—'

'How do you know this?'

'I know,' said Crag, 'because I was there. I didn't think much about it then ... I didn't think much about it afterwards. But it came to me at last that for a girl who had rushed me ... yes, Pippa, *rushed* me ... Rena was not following up that rush. I asked myself why, and I came up with this: It was because she didn't really want me and never had. She only wanted out from Uplands, away from Hardy. Because Hardy had said something that Rena had never experienced before. It was NO.'

'No to what?'

'No to Daddy's estate. No to all that Daddy's money could buy.'

'But, Crag, how can you say all this?'

'I heard it. I told you, Pippa. Rena had just suffered a fall from her hack ... Bunting, I remember. It was following one of her usual spats with Hardy about riding. It seems those two will always be horse-involved. I was riding with them. But it was Hardy who picked her up, and it was to Dom that she looked and said: "This is how it will be, won't it?" and he looked back at her and shook his head.

'It meant little to me then, but later, when she attached herself to me ... then attached herself to Glen Burt, I knew she was running away from something. Oh, this pride!' Crag shrugged his big shoulders.

'Yes, but Dom had it, too,' Pippa said loyally, loyal to Rena.

'But he put it aside when he came up here after her. And for that we have to thank old Franklin. If he hadn't altered his will like he did ... I often wonder, though, adoring Rena so much, that he—'

'I think,' said Pippa, 'I can explain that.' She told him of that last afternoon in Uncle Preston's sick-room, and how she had spoken of Dom as stubborn, proud and determined. How, later, when she had asked Uncle Preston was there anything he wanted, he had answered: 'You've given it to me.'

'So he clinched it by that will,' mused Crag. 'He knew that Dom would never agree to that will in a thousand years, so he kept an ember red and a fire alight. Though I think, Pippa, it could still have gone on and on but for the stallion. You know what, I'm glad about that wrong 'un, Bobby and all. After all, Bobby's no worse, in fact he's having a whale of a time in Minta, so we can say the wild feller saved Rena and Dom that thousand years,' he laughed.

Pippa said thoughtfully, 'You're fond of that number, aren't you? In fact Rupie and Davy intend questioning you about it again. You wrote it down in an order. A thousand candles.'

'Put into gross they wouldn't sound so crazy,' Crag admitted whimsically. 'I'm sorry I've worried our two bookies.'

'Rupie was not so worried as puzzled. He reported that you'd said you'd always wanted them and there was no other way.'

'Sometimes I thought so, Pippa,' Crag said sadly. 'I thought that was only for people like my parents. – Do you remember?'

'Their love was a thousand candles,' Pippa remembered. She waited for him to go on.

'I knew the first light of a candle that day in the train to Tombonda. Ever since then they've been lighting up, one by one. But sometimes some went out' . . . he blew his cheeks, then puffed . . . 'you turned away.'

'You turned away yourself,' she came back hotly. 'You said "no ties tied" . . . "nothing" . . . "relax".'

'And every syllable seared me, killed me. But what else could I do, knowing—'

'Knowing, Crag?'

'That the scrubber had been between us. Oh, I loved him, Pippa, but—'

'But you're wrong,' she said quietly. 'Davy wasn't there. – Oh, Crag, are you quite mad?'

For the brown man was actually counting up . . . holding her tightly to him as he did so . . . skipping hundreds; he must be to reach 999 so soon.

'One thousand, Pippa. A thousand candles.'

She believed it. There was light everywhere.

GOLDEN HARLEQUIN LIBRARY

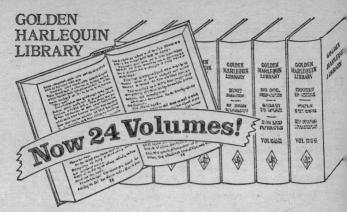

Now 24 Volumes!

Harlequin readers will be delighted! We've collected seventy two of your all-time favourite Harlequin Romance novels to present to you in an attractive new way. It's the Golden Harlequin Library.

Each volume contains three complete, unabridged Harlequin Romance novels, most of which have not been available since the original printing. Each volume is exquisitely bound in a fine quality rich gold hardcover with royal blue imprint. And each volume is priced at an unbelievable $1.75. That's right! Handsome, hardcover library editions at the price of paperbacks!

This very special collection of 24 volumes (there'll be more!) of classic Harlequin Romances would be a distinctive addition to your library. And imagine what a delightful gift they'd make for any Harlequin reader!

Start your collection now. See reverse of this page for full details.

SPECIAL INTRODUCTORY OFFER!

Order volumes No. 1, 2, 3, 4 and 5 now and get volume No. 6 FREE!

Just imagine . . . 18 unabridged HARLEQUIN ROMANCES beautifully bound in six library editions for only $8.75.